Flora Lyndsay

Or, Passages In An Eventful Life

Vol. II

by

Susanna Moodie

Double9 BOOKS

Flora Lyndsay

Or, Passages In An Eventful Life

Vol. II

by Susanna Moodie

ISBN: 978-93-70426-49-8

Published by

DOUBLE 9 BOOKS

2/13-B, Ansari Road
Daryaganj, New Delhi – 110002
info@double9books.com
www.double9books.com
Tel. 011-40042856

ABOUT THE AUTHOR

English-born Susanna Moodie, who lived in Canada from 6 December 1803 to 8 April 1885, wrote about her experiences as an immigrant in what was then a British province. On the banks of the River Waveney in Suffolk, Susanna Moodie was born in Bungay. In a family of authors that also included Agnes Strickland, Jane Margaret Strickland, and Catharine Parr Traill, she was the youngest sibling. In addition to publishing books about Spartacus and Jugurtha, she wrote her first children's book in 1822 and other children's stories in London. She participated in the Anti-Slavery Society in London and transcribed Mary Prince's story, a former slave from the Caribbean. She wed retired officer and Napoleonic War veteran John Moodie on 4 April 1831. Moodie immigrated to Upper Canada in 1832 together with her husband, a British Army officer, and daughter. Her brother Samuel Strickland (1804–1867) worked as a surveyor on a farm in Douro Township, close to Lakefield, north of Peterborough, where the family eventually lived. The farm now serves as a museum and houses antiquities. The museum, which Samuel founded, was formerly an Anglican church and has a view of Susanna's former canoeing spot on the Otonabee River.

CONTENTS

CHAPTER I
THE STATE CABIN

Why the apartment, into which Flora retreated on going on board was called a State-cabin, Flora could not imagine. It was really a very small closet, about seven feet in length, and a very little broader than it was long. It contained neither stool, bench, nor chair, and there was just room enough after closing the door, to turn round. The top of a large chest of painted deal drawers, with a raised board in front, and screened by faded red stuff curtains, formed the bed; for which Lyndsay had purchased a hair-mattress and feather pillows, to render it more comfortable during the voyage for his wife and child. This was perched up, however, at such an unreachable height from the ground, that the bed was on a level with Mrs. Lyndsay's chin.

"How in the world shall I ever get into it?" said Flora, appealing to her attendant in a tone half laughing, half crying. "If it is such a difficult thing now when the ship is at anchor, what will it be when she is plunging about in a storm?"

"You had better hax the capting, Marm. He must know the proper way of climbing up, for it was his own berth."

"That will seem so absurd. He may, however, have a step-ladder to reach it. Go to him, and ask him, with my compliments, how he gets into bed."

Hannah, returned laughing, and with flushed cheeks.

"La, Marm, he says 'that he gets in like other folks; that where there's a will there's allers a way.' An' he burst out into such a loud roaring laugh that it made me feel quite ashamed. Arter he had had his fun and wiped his eye—he has but one, you knows, Marm—he cries out, 'Hout! lass, let her jest make a flight of steps, by pulling out the drawers one above another for a little way. They answer the purpose of stairs, and if she's in downright earnest, she'll soon learn how to get in.'"

Flora was highly delighted with the result of Hannah's message. She immediately attempted the method proposed by the rough sailor, and after a trial or two, became quite expert in rolling in and out of the berth.

She now received a summons from the steward that "tea was ready."

"That's good news," said Hannah; "I feel quite raversome with hunger, and if I don't lay in a good stock to-night I shall feel bad enough to-morrow with the orrid sickness. The moment the ship begins to heave, I shall be heaving too."

"Say nothing about it, Hannah,—enjoy yourself while you can."

"There's company in the cabin, Marm,—not 'zactly ladies, but kind of ladies, such as Misses Waddel would call *decent* folk. One of them was sitting upon the Capting's knee when I went in, and drinking punch with him out of the same glass."

"Very *decent* ladies, truly," said Flora, doubtful whether to make one of such a refined party. Just as she had determined to remain where she was for the night, Lyndsay tapped at the door, and she called him in to hold a consultation.

"Come away," said he, laughing, "it is only the Captain's wife, and the mate's, with two of their sisters. Nice good-tempered women, who will behave themselves with due decorum. Old Boreas will be quite hurt, if you refuse to come out of your den, and play the amiable to his woman folk."

Flora no longer hesitated. She emerged from her hiding-place into the cabin, which now presented a very different appearance to what it had done some hours before. All the confusion of trunks and packages that had filled up the small available space had been removed, and it looked as neat and comfortable as such a confined crib could possibly look under the most favourable circumstances.

The company, consisting of four smartly-dressed young women, were ranged along the bench opposite the door from which Flora made her *débût*. They regarded her with a nervous, awkward agitation, as they rose simultaneously and dropped as low a courtesy as the narrow space between the bench and the table would allow. The ceremony of introduction then commenced, by the Captain rising to his legs, and stretching out his red, right hand with an air of dignity, "Mrs. Lyndsay, cabin passenger in the brig *Anne*—Mrs. Williams, my wife, Ma'am,—Mrs. Collins, Mrs. Lyndsay,—my wife's sister-in-law,—Miss Nancy and Betsy Collins, Mrs. Lyndsay,—Mr. Collins, my first mate, and brother to Mrs. Williams, Mrs. Lyndsay."

Then came the shaking of hands. Lyndsay, who observed the embarrassment of the family party assembled in the cabin, received them with a frank courtesy, which soon restored confidence, and set them at their ease; though it was difficult to refrain from a smile at the scared look they cast at each other when Mrs. Lyndsay took her seat among them; and the dead silence which fell upon them, and checked the lively chattering that a few minutes before had rung through the cabin.

Tea and coffee were smoking upon the table, which was covered with all sorts of dainties, which the captain's wife had brought in a basket to make merry with, and which she proffered to the strangers with true Scotch hospitality, assuring them that the rich bun and short-bread had been made with her *ain* hands, as a little treat for Jock before leaving the country.

"Meg forgets that I'm a rough English sailor, and don't care a fig for her Scotch sunkets," quoth Boreas, speaking with his mouth full of short bread. "A good red herring and a slice of Gloster cheese is worth them all. But wilful women will have their own way, and I must eat the mawkish trash to please her."

"An' find it varra gude, Jock, an' I'm no mistaken," said the buxom fair-haired woman, tapping his rough cheek. "It wad be something new for him to praise onything made by his ain wife."

And then she rattled away about the inconstancy of men, and of sailors especially, in such a droll, provoking manner, that she forced her rude lord to lay aside his dignity and laugh at her nonsense. She was a comely, sonsy dame, neither very young, nor very pretty; but he was her senior by many years, and he bore her raillery with the same grace that a staid old cat submits to the impertinent caresses and cuffs of a frolicsome kitten. When he growled and swore, she clapped her hands and laughed, and called him her dear old sea-bear, and hoped that he would not die of grief during her absence.

"Never fear, Meg, I don't mean to give you the chance of tormenting another fellow out of his wits. I shall live long enough to plague you yet."

"Na doubt," said Meg, "which thought will console me for your absence; an' I sall be as merry as a lark until you return to execute your threat."

"Meg, you are a daft woman," said Collins, the mate. "The captain does na half like your teasing. Can't you leave him alone?"

"Mind your ain business, Wullie, an' take care of your ain wife. I canna play the fule like Jean, wha's whimperin' by hersel in the corner."

This was indeed the case. Mrs. Collins had only been married a few weeks, and the parting with her bridegroom was a heart-breaking affair.

They were a very interesting young couple; and the tall, fair girl sat apart from the rest of the group, nursing an agony of fear in her gentle breast, lest her Willie should be drowned, and she should never see him again. She made desperate efforts to control her grief, and conceal the tears that rolled in quick succession down her pale cheeks. Collins sprang to her side, and circling her slender waist with his manly arm, whispered into her ears loving words, full of hope and comfort. It would not do: the poor girl could not be reconciled to the separation, and answered all his tender endearments with low, stifled sobs, filling the heart of the lover husband, with the grief which burthened her own.

Collins had a fine sensible face, though it had been considerably marred by the small-pox. His features were straight and well-cut, his hair dark and curling, his handsome grey eyes full of manly fire. Though not exactly a gentleman, he possessed high and honourable feelings, and his frank manners and independent bearing won for him the goodwill and respect of all.

Doubtless Jean thought him the handsomest man in a' Scotland; and most women would have said that he was a good-looking dashing sailor. As he bent over his disconsolate weeping bride, with such affectionate earnest love beaming from his fine eyes, and tried with gentle words to reconcile her to their inevitable parting, he afforded a striking contrast to his superior, who regarded a temporary absence from his spouse as a thing of course,—a mere matter of business, which he bore with his usual affectation of stubborn indifference.

Feeling that her presence must be a restraint upon the family party, the moment the evening meal was concluded Flora bade them good night, and retired to her *state* cabin, worn out with the fatigue of the day. The rain was still falling heavily, and she was forced to leave her door partly unclosed to obtain a little air, for the heat was oppressive in the close confined berth. For a long time she lay awake, now thinking sad thoughts and shedding sadder tears, now listening to the hum of voices in the outer-cabin, broken occasionally by songs and merry bursts of laughter.

The captain's wife and her sisters, she found, were on their way to Anster fair, which was to be held on the morrow, at which place they were to be put on shore. And she remembered the old song of Maggie Lauder, and her encounter with the piper on her way to that celebrated fair: and was not a little amused to hear old Boreas, as if he had read her thoughts, roar out the national ditty in a hoarse deep voice, as rough and unmusical as a nor-wester piping among the shrouds.

As she reclined on her pillow, she could just see through a small aperture in the red curtains which concealed her person from observation the party gathered around the cabin-table. The captain's wife was seated on his knee, and Jean's pale cheek rested on her bridegroom's manly breast. Old Boreas was in his glory, for the brandy bottle was before him, and he was insisting upon the ladies taking a glass of punch, and drinking success to the voyage. This they all did with a very *good grace*; even the pensive Jean sipping occasionally from her husband's tumbler.

The captain's wife began teasing him for a fairing, which he very bluntly refused to bestow. She called in the aid of Miss Nancy and Betsy, and they charged down upon him with such a din of voices, that the jolly tar emptied the contents of his leathern purse into Meg's lap, who clutched the silver and kissed him, and clapped his broad back, and laughed like a child.

By-and-by he was forced to leave her to go upon deck. She then rose and went to her brother, and laying her hand upon his shoulder, addressed him in a manner so serious, so different from her former deportment, that Flora could scarcely believe it was the same person that now spoke.

"Wullie, ye maun promise me to keep a gude look out on Jock during the voyage. He's jest killin' o' himsel wi' drink. Canna ye persuade him to gie it up ava?"

The mate shook his head. "Ye ken the man, Maggie. He wull gang his ain gate."

Maggie sighed heavily. "It's a puir look-out for his wife an' the twa weans. He'll no leave it aff for our sakes; but you maun put in a word o' advice now and then."

"It's of na use, Maggie. He's as obstinate as a brute beast. If he wull na do it for your sake and the bairns—he'll no be convinced by word o' mine. I'm thinkin', that opposition on that heid wud do mair harm than gude."

"An' then, they women folk—Wullie. He's na to be trusted. Wi' him—out o' sight is out o' mind. He never thinks o' his wife at hame the moment he puts out to sea."

"Dinna be sae jealous, woman. Ha' ye na faith?" said Collins, pressing Jean closer to his heart "Do ye think that sailors ar' waur than ither men?"

"Ye are a' alike," sighed Meg, "though doubtless Jean thinks ye wull ever be true to her, an' keep your eyes shut when you pass a pretty lass for her sake. I ken you better."

"I were nae worthy to be your brither's wife, Maggie, an' I doubted his honesty," said Jean indignantly, as she lifted her long, fair curls from her husband's breast, and regarded him with a glance of proud devotion. "If ye had mair faith in Jock, he wu'd be a better man."

"It's early days wi' ye yet, Jean;—wait a wee while afore ye find faut wi' yer elders. Wullie weel kens, that I'm na mistrustfu' wi'out cause."

Flora did not hear the mate's reply: sleep weighed heavily upon her eyelids, and she dropped off into profound repose.

CHAPTER II
FLORA'S FELLOW-PASSENGERS

The grey dawn glimmered faintly through the bull's-eye of ground glass in the ceiling of Mrs. Lyndsay's cabin, before she again unclosed her eyes. She sat up in her berth and steadied herself, glancing at first wonderingly around her, and marvelling where she was. The heaving of the vessel, and the quick rushing of the waves against her sides, informed her that the ship had sailed during the night, and recalled to her mind the events of the past day.

The voyage, whether for good or ill, had commenced; and the certainty of her present position relieved her mind of a heavy burden of anxiety. She rose and dressed herself, and earnestly besought the Almighty to protect them from the perils and dangers of the deep, and watch over them for good during their passage across the mighty waters. Strengthened and refreshed by this act of devotion, she felt her spirits revive and her heart expand with renewed cheerfulness and hope, and trustfully believed that God had given a favourable answer to her prayer.

Early as the hour was, she found watchful eyes awake in the ship. The Captain was already on deck, and Sam Fraser, the Steward, a smart lad of eighteen, was cleaning out the cabin. The boards felt cold and wet, and Flora, who was anxious to see all she could of the coast of Scotland, hurried upon deck, where she found her husband up before her, conversing with the Captain.

The *Anne*, with all her white sails set, was scudding before a favourable wind, which whistled aloft strange solemn anthems in the shrouds. The sun had just climbed above the mountain-heights, that formed a glorious background to the blue glancing waters, over which the ship glided like a thing of life. It was a splendid July morning, and the white-crested billows flashed and rolled their long sparkling surges beneath a sky of cloudless brilliancy. All nature glowed with life and beauty, as land and sea looked up rejoicingly, to hail the broad, open eye of day.

"Twas heaven above—around—below."

The romantic features of the coast, with all the poetical and historical associations connected with it, the deep music of ocean, the very smell of the salt brine, filled the heart of Flora Lyndsay with hope and joy. To have gazed upon such a soul-stirring scene with a mind burdened with painful regrets, would have been an act of impiety towards the bountiful Creator, whose presence is never more fully recognised than when following the course that His wisdom has shaped out for us across that pathless wilderness of waves,—that wonderful mirror of His power, that, whether in storm or shine, faithfully reflects the glory and greatness of its Maker.

With returning health and spirits, Flora's mind recovered its former tone. She felt not only contented, but happy, and submitted herself with child-like confidence to the protecting care of the universal Father.

All, doubtless, she thought, is ordained for the best. If not for us, for our children. Others have toiled for us; it is but right that we should toil in our turn. It is to the workers, not to the dreamers, that earth opens up her treasures. Life is beset with trials, take which path we may. The brightest sky at times is darkened by clouds; the calmest ocean vexed with storms. What matters it that we are called upon to bear the burden and heat of the day, if we receive the reward of our labours at night? If the sunset be fair and peaceful, who recals the tempest that darkened the heavens at noon? The quiet grave receives all at last; and those who have worked hardest on earth, will find a brighter morning for their eternal holiday of love and praise.

"What are you thinking of, Flora?" said Lyndsay, drawing her arm within his own.

"I was thinking, dearest, that it was good to be here."

"Your thoughts, then, were an echo of my own. Depend upon it, Flora, that we shall find it all right at last."

For a long time they stood together, silently surveying the magnificent coast which was rapidly gliding from them. Lyndsay's soul-lighted eyes rested proudly upon it; and a shade of melancholy passed across his brow. It was his native land, and he deeply felt that he looked upon its stern majestic face for the last time; but he was not a man who could impart the inner throbbings of his heart, (and it was a great heart,) to others. Such feelings he considered too sacred to unveil to common observation; and even she could only read by the varying expression of his countenance the thoughts that were working within.

"Courage, my dear Flora," he said at length, with one of his own kind smiles. "All will be well in the end; and we shall still be happy in each other's love. Yes, as happy in the backwoods of Canada, as we have been in England."

Flora felt that with him she could be happy anywhere; that paradise would be a prison, if his presence did not enliven and give interest to the scene.

Few of the emigrants had found their way to the deck at that early hour; and for some time Flora enjoyed a charming *tête-à-tête* with her husband. Gradually the deck grew more populous; and men were seen lounging against the bulwarks, smoking their pipes, or performing their ablutions, a wooden tub and canvass bucket serving them for hand-basin and water-jug.

Tom afterwards commenced the great business of cooking the morning meal; and Hannibal, the black lord of the caboose, was beset by a host of scolding, jabbering women, all fighting and quarrelling for the first chance at the stove. He took their abuse very coolly, settling the dispute by making the auld wives draw lots for precedence. They consented to this arrangement with a very bad grace. Not more than four kettles could occupy the fire at one time, and though some clubbed, and made their mess of porridge together in one large pot, the rest grumbled and squabbled during the whole operation, elbowing and crowding for more room, and trying to push each other's coffee and teapots into the fire. And then all in a breath, at the very top of their shrill voices, appealed to Hannibal to act as umpire among them, and establish their claims to the best side of the fire. His answer was brief and to the point—

"Dere be dis fire. You hab him so long. Him wait for no one. Your time up. You take off pot, or I pitch pot into sea. Others must eat as well as you; so keep your breath to cool your porridge; and if that no suit you, fight it out—fight it out!"

Here he flourished over their heads his iron ladle, full of some scalding liquor, which silenced the combatants for one while, until a new set of applicants emerging from the gangway, made them rush more vigorously than ever to the charge.

As Flora continued pacing the deck, and watching the noisy group round the cooking-stove, she felt no small degree of curiosity respecting them. They were her fellow-voyagers to that unknown land to which all their hopes and fears instinctively turned; and she could scarcely regard with indifference those whom Providence had thrown together in pursuit of the same object. She wanted to know something about them from their own lips—what their past lives had been, what were their future prospects, and the causes that had led them to emigrate to Canada.

Perhaps something of the same feeling is experienced by most persons suddenly thrown together and confined for some weeks in such a narrow space as the interior of a small brig, for the *Anne* contained more passengers for her size and tonnage than many large three-masted vessels. During the long voyage her curiosity was amply gratified, and she learned something of the history and characters of most of these people. First, there was an old highland soldier, who had served during the greater part of the Peninsular war, and had seen a great deal of hard service, and received a number of hard knocks in the way of wounds and broken bones, of which (now the pain and danger was over) he was not a little proud, as they formed a never-ending theme of boasting and self-exaltation; and had honest Donald Macdonald charged his fellow-passengers a penny a peep at the scars on his legs, breast, and arms, he might have made enough to pay the expenses of his passage out. "His wounds," he said, "were all in the right place. He was too well bred to turn his back to an enemy."

Macdonald was one of the many unfortunate old pensioners, who had been induced to part with a certain provision for his old age, to try his fortunes in the backwoods of Canada. He knew as little of hard labour as any officer in his regiment, still less of agricultural pursuits; and perhaps could barely have told the difference between one sort of grain and another, having entered the army a mere boy, quite raw and inexperienced, from his native hills.

He had a wife, and five rude, brawny, coarse children—the three eldest girls from seven to fourteen years of age. "They were not of the right sort," he said; "but they were strong enough for boys, and would make fine mothers for dragoons to serve in case of war."

But as Canada is not at all a warlike country, these qualifications in his bouncing, red haired lassies, were no recommendation. The two spoilt boys were still in short coats, and could afford little help to their veteran father for many years to come.

Donald had formed the most extravagant notions of Canada. In his eyes it was a perfect El Dorado, where gold was as plentiful as blackberries upon the bushes. He did not seem ever to have given the idea of having to work for his living a thought—and laughed at a notion so disagreeable and repugnant to his old habits, as absurd.

"Whar was the use of ganging to a new country," he said, "if a bodie had to work as hard there as in the auld?"

After paying his passage-money, and furnishing provisions for the voyage, he had only the sum of nineteen pounds remaining, which he considered an inexhaustible fund of wealth, from which he was to obtain, not only a comfortable living in the land of promise, but an independent fortune. He was entitled to a grant of land, which he said, "Would make him a laird, and place him on an equal footing with the lairds in the backwoods of Canada."

Flora often wondered in after years, what became of poor Macdonald and all his high-flown dreams of future greatness.

The wife of the old soldier was a tall, raw-boned, red-fisted virago, who fought with both fists and tongue. She seemed to live in a perfect element of strife. A quarrel could not exist in the ship without her being either the original cause, or the active promoter of it, after it was once set on foot. She would bully the captain, out-swear the sailors, and out-scold all the rest of the femalities in the vessel.

The daughter of a soldier, born amidst the horrors of war, and brought up as a camp-follower, her ignorance of all the gentler humanities of life was only exceeded by her violence. While assisting in pillaging the dead, after the battle of Waterloo, she had found the sum of a hundred gold Napoleons concealed in a belt upon the person of a dead French officer. This made her a woman of fortune, and led to her marriage with her present husband, for she had had several, who doubtless were glad to be released by death from the unnatural tyranny of such a mate. Macdonald was an easy, good-natured man, who for the sake of peace, let the wilful woman have her own way, and thrash him and the bairns as often as the wicked spirit by which she was possessed, prompted her to exhibit these peculiar marks of her conjugal and maternal love.

Had Macdonald been asked, why he submitted to such base treatment from his wife, he might have answered with the tall Canadian backwoodsman, when questioned on the same subject,—

"It pleases her, and it don't hurt I."

Mrs. Macdonald was in a delicate situation, and from the very day the ship sailed, she gave out that she was on the eve of an increase to her interesting family: to the great indignation of the captain, who had a mortal antipathy to babies, and who declared in his rough way, "That it was an imposition; Mrs. Macdonald had no right to swindle him into taking out more passengers than he had bargained for."

The stalwart dame was enchanted that she had found out a way to annoy the captain, to whose orders she was forced to submit, and whom in consequence she regarded as a bitter enemy. In fact she did all in her power to encourage his fears respecting her. Whenever he paced the deck in sullen dignity, she began to sigh and groan, and declare in a voice loud enough for him to overhear, "That she did na think that she could haud out anither day ava'."

There was another pensioner on board who was the sworn friend and countryman of Macdonald. Hugh Mackenzie was a dragoon, and a fine tall, soldierly-looking man. His wife was a little, chatty, gossiping woman, from Berwickshire; a good creature in her way, but sadly addicted to the use of strong waters, drowning the little sense she had in the fumes of whiskey and brandy. She and her husband spent all their time in eating and drinking, when they were not taking snuff and smoking. They were cooking, or preparing for it, from morning till night; and generally headed the forlorn hope which three times a day besieged the caboose, and defied the valiant Hannibal to his very teeth.

Mrs. Mackenzie was the very reverse of her gude friend, Mrs. Macdonald; for she stood in perpetual fear of her tall husband, who thrashed her soundly when she got drunk. Moreover, she was very jealous of all the young women in the ship, whom she termed, "Lazy, bold, gude for nought hizzies, who wud na led a' bodies ain man alane."

She would sit for hours on the deck smoking a short black pipe, and crooning old border ballads, in a voice anything but musical.

During Flora's long morning promenade upon deck, she more than once caught a pair of yellow, queer-looking eyes peering at her from beneath the shade of one of the boats which were slung to the main-mast, and by-and-by a singularly disagreeable-looking head raised itself from a couch of cloaks, and continued its investigation in a very intrusive manner. The head belonged to a little man in a snuff-coloured suit, whose small, pert, pugnacious face, eyes, hair and complexion, were only a variety of the same shades as the dress in which he had cased his outer man. Flora quietly pointed him out to her husband, and asked in a whisper, "What he thought of the little brown man?"

"His appearance is not at all prepossessing," said Lyndsay. "I will ask the Captain, who is coming this way, who and what he is?"

The question seemed to embarrass old Boreas not a little. He threw a frowning glance towards the spot occupied by the stranger, shrugged his shoulders, whistled a tune, and thrusting his hands into his breeches' pockets, took several turns on the deck before he made any reply. Until, seeing the snuff-coloured individual about to crawl out of his hiding-place, he called out in a gruff voice—

"Keep where you are, Sir—the longer you remain out of sight the better. By exposing yourself to observation, you may cause trouble to more persons than *one*!"

The person thus unceremoniously addressed, smiled malignantly, and retreating beneath the shade of the boat, snarled out some reply, only audible to the captain; whose advice did not however seem lost upon him, for after the Lyndsays had taken another turn or two, and he had glared at them with his little fiery eyes, sufficiently to gratify his insolent curiosity, he again emerged from under the boat, and succeeded in tumbling into it. Drawing a part of a spare sail over his diminutive person, he vanished as completely from sight, as if the ocean had suddenly swallowed him up.

"I was a d——d fool!" muttered the captain, returning to Lyndsay's side, "to let that fellow, with his ugly, sneering phiz, come on board! But as he is here, I must make the best of a bad bargain. You will not peach, so I'll just give you a bit of his history, and explain the necessity of his keeping close until we are out of the sight of land. Hang him! his ugly phiz is enough to sink the ship. Had I seen him before he came on board, he might have rotted in gaol before I took charge of his carcase. And then, 'tis such a conceited ass, he will take no advice, and cares as little for his own safety as he does for mine."

"Is he a runaway felon?" asked Flora.

"You have not made a bad guess, Mistress Lyndsay. He was a distiller, who carried on a good business in Edinburgh. He cheated the Government, and was cashiered for a large sum, more than he could pay by a long chalk. His friends contrived his escape, and smuggled him on board last night, just as the anchor was being weighed. They offered me a handsome sum to carry him to Quebec. Should he be discovered by any of the passengers before we lose sight of the British coast, he would be seized when the ship puts into Kirkwall, and that would be a bad job for us both. The transaction is entirely between his friends and me; Mr. Gregg knows nothing about it."

"And are we to have the pleasure of his company in the cabin during the voyage?"

"That would be bad indeed. No, he has a berth provided for him in the store-room, and has the privilege of having his grub sent to him from the cabin-table, and the use of the tea and coffeepot after we have done with it. This is quite good enough for a rogue like him. But I hear Sam Frazer hallooing for breakfast. Come down to the cabin, Mrs. Lyndsay, the sea air must have made you hungry."

The little cabin was in apple-pie order. A clean diaper cloth covered the table, on which the common crockery, cups and saucers were arranged with mathematical precision, while the savoury smell of fried fish and hot coffee, promised the hungry emigrants a substantial breakfast.

On inquiring for Hannah and James Hawke, Flora found that both were confined to their berths with sea-sickness. Old Boreas complimented her not a little on her being able to appear at the breakfast-table. The fish proved excellent; the coffee, a black, bitter compound, which Flora drank with a very ill grace. The captain, with an air of exultation, produced from his own private cupboard, which formed the back panelling of his berth, a great stone jar of milk, which his wife had prepared with sugar to last him the voyage.

"Have you no cow on board?" asked Flora, rather anxiously, for little Josey and her comfort was always uppermost in her mind.

"Cow! Who the devil would be bothered with a cow," said Boreas, "when he can procure a substitute like this. Here's my dun cow; she'll give us what we want without the trouble of milking. Won't she, Sam?" appealing to his steward, to second his assertion.

"Yes, Sir," and Sam grinned applause. "But I'm jist thinkin', Captain, that the weather's o'er hot, an' the dun cow may gang drie afore we see Canada."

The captain's cow turned out a very sorry animal, for in less than two days the milk was so putrid, that it had to be thrown overboard, and his cabin-passengers were forced to drink the vile coffee, and still viler tea, without milk, during the rest of the voyage, with only coarse brown sugar to soften its disagreeable flavour.

It must be confessed, that the cabin bill of fare presented no tempting variety. After the first week the fresh mutton and beef was changed to salt pork and hard junk, ship biscuit and peas, and potatoes of the last year's growth, rancid butter, and oatmeal porridge, with porter and brown sugar for sauce; and sometimes—but this was a very great dainty—a slice of Dunlop cheese. Nothing but hunger, and constant exercise upon the deck in the open air, reconciled Mrs. Lyndsay to this coarse diet. It was not what they had been promised; but complaints were useless. There certainly was no danger of hurting their health by over indulgence, as it was with difficulty they could satisfy their hunger with the unpalatable fare, which was old, and not even good of its kind.

The Lyndsays were always glad when the homely meal was over, and they could escape once more to the deck, and enjoy the fine coast views, and the fresh invigorating sea breeze.

CHAPTER III
THE LAST GLANCE OF SCOTLAND

The weather for the next three days continued as fine as summer weather could be. With wind and tide in her favour, the *Anne* made a splendid run through the Moray Firth, passed the auld town of Aberdeen, and before sunset sailed close under the dreary Caithness coast.

Flora examined John o' Groat's house with some interest, and for the first time in her life discovered that the fantastic red rock which bears that name, was not a *bonâ fide* dwelling, which up to that moment she had imagined it to be.

A prospect more barren and desolate than that over which Caithness Castle rises preeminent, can scarcely be imagined. Flora turned from the contemplation of the stony waste with an inward thanksgiving, "That it was not her home." But when they rounded Duncansby Head, the scene before so tame and sterile, became more grand and picturesque every moment. They were now in the stormy Pentland Firth, threading their way with the aid of a pilot through its romantic labyrinth of islands, driven onward by a spanking wind.

The bold outline of the coast was so different in its character from that to which she had been accustomed from a child, that it made a powerful impression upon her mind, and quickly associated itself with all the legends of the wild and marvellous which she had ever heard or read. Those beetling crags, those ocean caves, into which the wild sea-waves rushed with such a fearful din, seemed fitting habitations for all the evil demons that abound in the Scandinavian mythology, once dreaded as stern realities in a darker stage of human progression.

How tame beside these awful sublimities, appeared the gentle sloping cliffs at ——, and her little cottage fronting the quiet bay—

"Green lie these thickly timbered shores,
Fair sloping to the sea."

But here, rocks upon rocks in endless confusion, reared their craggy heads towards heaven, their frowning shadows casting a Stygian gloom upon the billows that leap and roar around their massive base. A perpetual war of ages these billows have waged against the iron barrier, that with silent, motionless, resistless force repels their white-crested phalanx, scattering them into shining fragments of snowy spray. Ocean will not be defeated—he calls his legions again and again to the charge, only to be broken and beaten back as before. They retreat with a sullen roar of defiance, that seems to say, "You have beaten us; but we will try our strength against you once more. The day is coming when one of us two must yield."

The rocks assumed all hues in the fiery beams of the setting sun. The red granite glowed with tints of crimson, violet, indigo, and gold, these colours assuming a greater intensity when reflected in the transparent waters of the Firth. It was a scene to see, not prate about, and the memory of its brilliancy still lies enshrined like some precious gem in Flora Lyndsay's heart.

As headland after headland flew past, revealing at every point some fresh combinations of grandeur and beauty, Flora clapped her hands together in a sort of ecstasy.

Lyndsay was standing silently beside her, watching with an air of melancholy interest the scene which excited in her such intense enthusiasm.

"Flora, do you see that old-fashioned mansion that crowns the green amphitheatre, surrounded by those lofty hills, in front of us? It is a lovely romantic place—with that giant hill that looks like an old man in a highland bonnet, towering above it, away there in the back-ground. That is the old man of Hoy. That old house is M— —, where I was born and brought up." He drew a deep sigh, and turning his face from his wife, continued to gaze with an earnest longing. The shades of night drew a veil over the stern landscape, and the moon rose up, bathing rock and crag and mountain height with a flood of silver glory, and adding a ghostlike awful sublimity to the scene. Lyndsay still leant upon the vessel's side, watching with the same intense expression the black outline of the receding coast, which in that uncertain light presented an aspect of rugged frowning desolation.

The Captain expected to put into Kirkwall, at which place he had been requested by the owners to take in a supply of fresh provisions and water for the voyage; the water casks having been filled with the execrable waters o' Leith, under the ostensible reason of keeping them from leaking until they could obtain a better supply. But the wind and tide being in his favour, and enabling him to make a rapid run through the Firth, he thought it best to keep straight on. This, in the end, by leaving the vessel short of provisions and water, proved a short-sighted policy, while it greatly disappointed Flora, whom Lyndsay had promised to introduce to some of his friends, and give her a nearer view of the romantic islands, which, seen from the water, had excited her curiosity to the utmost.

But the *Anne* spread her white wings to catch the fresh breeze which was piping its hoarse song among the shrouds, and sped far upon her westward way, leaving Mrs. Lyndsay to upbraid the Captain with having cheated her hopes, which now could never be realized.

Boreas only laughed, and said—"That he was d——d sorry, for that he would have to drink bad water and eat salt junk the rest of the voyage."

"And what has become of the little man in brown?" asked Flora: "I have not seen him since he crept into the boat."

"We had a blow up this morning," said Boreas. "When I came on deck, my gentleman was marching about as bold as you please, and had the impudence to threaten to kick one of the emigrant children overboard, if he found him in his path again. When I remonstrated with the scoundrel on his impudence, as the father of the child knew him, and might report him to the pilot, he bade me 'Go to h——, and take care of my own people. He would not submit to my low tyranny. He would do as he pleased, without asking my leave!' And then the fellow began to rave and swear in such an outrageous manner, that I could hardly resist the inclination I felt to pitch him plump into the sea. But I had my revenge. Ha! ha! I had my revenge."

"In what way?" asked Lyndsay.

"The best way in the world; and the snarling puppy had no one to blame but himself. My dog Oscar is d——d ugly, but he's the most sagacious beast in the world. He can tell an honest man at a glance, and he hates rogues. Oscar sat on his haunches eyeing the little man, with no very amiable squint, during the row; every now and then uttering a significant growl, and making a preparatory snap at Mr. Lootie's legs, as if he longed to take the quarrel under his own especial management. In the heat of anger, Mr. Lootie kept raising his hands and shaking them at me in a threatening manner. Oscar let it pass for what it was worth the first time, but the moment the fist was raised a second time, he dashed into the little brute with tooth and claw, and pulling him to the ground, he gave him such a touzling that the distiller was fain to roar aloud for mercy, and I proved just then very deaf, and he got enough of it, I can tell you."

"He was rightly served," said Flora; "I expect he will afford us some amusement during the voyage. Captain, where did you procure this cod-fish? I never tasted anything so delicious in the fish way in my life."

"Ah, I thought you'd find that a treat. Those fish were alive under the blue waters of the Firth an hour ago. Talk of the fine flavour of the

Newfoundland cod! they are not comparable to the fish caught in these rapid waters."

Flora was on deck by sunrise the next morning. The sky was still cloudless, but the breeze had freshened and the sea was coveted with short rolling billows, which recalled to her mind a beautiful line in Ossian, where the old bard compares these white-crested, short waves to a flock of sheep coming tumbling over one another from the hills; and in another place he terms the wind that moves them—

"The shepherdess of the sea driving her flocks on shore."

A tall, dark man, that was at the wheel, and bore the very appropriate name of Bob *Motion*, whether real or assumed, it would be hard to say; called this short chopping sea, "The white mice being out."

Flora found it no easy matter to keep her feet on the deck while the vessel was going sideways through the water, but she hung on to the bulwarks, and was rewarded by the sight of the wild Sutherland coast on the left, its brown heath-covered hills, and fantastic rocks, conjuring up the form of the Norna of the fitful Head—

"And of every wild shore that the northern winds knew."

Very few of the emigrants had ventured out of the steerage, being down with sea-sickness; but Flora never suffered once from this distressing malady during the voyage. This morning, in particular, she felt well and in high spirits—a sense of glorious freedom in thus bounding over the free, glad waves, in feeling their spray upon her lips, and the fresh wild breath of the wind fanning her cheek, and whistling through her hair. The ship seemed endowed with life as well as motion, as she leaped from wave to wave, and breasted the flashing brine as if it were her servant, and sworn to do her bidding.

"Well, Flora, what do you think of Lord Rae's country?" said Lyndsay.

"It is terrific!" returned Flora; "I cannot look at that confusion of hills, lifting their tall heads to heaven, but I fancy that the earth has rebelled against her Maker, and dares to defy Him to his face. It is odd—a strange madness, you will think—but the sight of these mountains thrills me with fear. I feel myself grow pale while looking at them, and tremble while I admire."

"To me, born among the hills, Flora, these sensations of yours are almost incomprehensible. But look, that broken arch of stone formed by those immense black rocks round which the wild waves revel, and leap in a glad frenzy, is the entrance to Loch Gribol. It is one of the grandest objects on this rugged coast."

How often amid the dark woods of Canada did the stern sublimity of that awful scene return to Flora Lyndsay in her dreams! The barren coast of Anticosti, the pine-covered precipices of freestone that frown over Chaleur Bay, and the mountain range which extends on the north of the St. Lawrence from the Gulf to Quebec, though they present every variety of savage scenery, cannot compete with the lonely, sterile grandeur which marks the dashing of the ocean waves into that Highland loch.

The long, bright summer day wore to its close, and before the moon looked down upon the heath-clad hills, the lighthouse on Cape Wrath had diminished to a star amid the waves, and the coast of Scotland looked like a dim wreath of blue smoke upon the verge of the horizon.

The little islands of Barra and Rona dimly distinguished above the waves, were the last of the British Isles which met Flora's anxious glance; and when they faded into the immensity of ocean, and were lost to sight, and the vessel fairly stood to sea, a sense of loneliness, of perpetual exile, pressed so heavily upon her heart, that she left the deck, and sought her bed, that she might bewail in solitude her last passionate adieu to her native land.

CHAPTER IV
STEPHEN CORRIE

Now that the fear of detection was over, the little brown man fearlessly emerged from his hiding-place in the boat, and promenaded the deck from morning till night, sneering at the steerage-passengers, and abusing the sailors in the most arrogant and assured manner.

He was the most contrary, malicious, waspish elf that could well be imagined. If he could not find an opportunity for stinging and teasing with his ill-natured sarcasms and remarks, he buzzed around his victims like an irritated musquito, whose shrill notes of defiance and antagonism are as bad as its bite. The more Flora saw of Mr. Lootie the less she wished to see of him; but she could not come upon the deck without his pestering her with his company, and annoying her with observations on his fellow-passengers, which were as unjust as they were cruel.

It was in vain that she turned her back upon him, and gave him curt ungracious answers, often affecting not to hear him at all. The little snuff-coloured man was too much at heart a sneak, with all his impudence, to be readily shook off.

It was only when Oscar, who had attached himself to Mrs. Lyndsay and her child, accompanied her to the deck, that Mr. Lootie kept his distance. The fierce terrier had only to draw up his lip and show his ivories, hissing through them a short ominous snarl, and the brown dwarf retreated with a growl and a curse into his boat.

I am sorry to say that Flora actually fostered the deadly enmity which existed between Oscar and the recreant distiller, which seemed the more unjustifiable, as there was a positive personal likeness between the biped and the quadruped. They had the same short, pert contour of face, the same petulant curl of the nostrils, the same fiery red flash in the small yellow brown eyes, and the very same method of snarling and showing off their white malicious-looking teeth. The very colour of Oscar's low rough coat was nearly the same as the scanty beard and hair of his inveterate foe. Could Oscar have spoken with a human tongue, he would have declared himself very little flattered by the resemblance; for rough as he was, he was an honest dog, and loved honesty in others. There was only one mental feature common to both—their capacity to hate and to annoy those they disliked.

Occasionally the little brown man indulged in a fit of mirth. When retreating under the shade of his ark of safety, the boat, he would sing in a low bow-wow tone some ditty only known to himself, the upper notes of which resembled a series of continued snarls. Oscar would then stop just in front of him, and snarl in return, till the patience of the musician was utterly exhausted, and he would rush out of his hiding-place, and pursue his hairy foe round the deck with a cudgel, uttering unmistakeable curses at every blow.

These skirmishes were nuts for old Boreas to crack, who putting his arms akimbo, would encourage the pugnacity of his dog with loud cries:

"At him, Oscar!—at him! Give it him strong, my boy!" to the no small indignation of Mr. Lootie, who would retire, muttering to himself—

"I don't know which is the greatest brute of the two, you or your cur!"

"My dog is a good physiognomist; he knows best," would be the rejoinder; and the war would recommence with greater fury than ever.

Mr. Lootie was not the only mysterious passenger on board the brig *Anne*. There was another, who made his appearance among the steerage passengers the moment the vessel was out of sight of land, to the astonishment of old Boreas and his crew—a young, handsome, dare-devil sort of a chap, who might have numbered six-and-twenty years, who called himself Stephen Corrie. He made his *débût* upon deck as suddenly and as unexpectedly as if he had fallen from the stars, and possessed the power of rendering himself visible or invisible at will.

No one knew, or pretended to know, who he was, or from whence he came. He had been smuggled on board by the women folk. It was their secret, and, though it must have been known to many of them, they kept it well.

No luggage had he to encumber the hold, not a copper in his pockets, not a change of raiment for his back; the clothes he wore, being of the lightest and cheapest description. A checked shirt and coarse white canvass jacket and trowsers, comprised his whole wardrobe. He had laid in no provisions for the voyage, but lived upon the contributions of the poor emigrants, with whom he was the most popular man on board, and no one was better fed, or seemed to enjoy better health or spirits. The latter commodity appeared perfectly inexhaustible. He laughed and sung, told long yarns, and made love to all the young women, whose especial darling and idol he seemed to be. The first on deck, and the last to leave, he was a living embodiment of the long-sought-for principle of perpetual motion: his legs and tongue never seemed to tire, and his loud, clear voice and joyous peals of laughter, rang unceasingly through the ship. When not singing, whistling, shouting, or making fun for all around him, he danced hornpipes, making his fingers keep time with his feet, by a continual snapping, which resembled the strokes of the tambourine or castanets. A more mercurial jovial fellow never set old Time at defiance, or laughed in the grisly face of Care.

Tall and lithe of limb, his complexion was what the Scotch term *sandy*; his short curling hair and whiskers resembling the tint of red gravel, profuse in quantity, fine in quality, and clustering round his high, white forehead with most artistic grace. His features were both regular and well-cut, his large bright blue eyes overflowing with mirth and reckless audacity. When he laughed, which was every other minute, he showed a dazzling set of snow-white teeth, and looked so happy and free from care, that every one laughed with him, and echoed the droll sayings which fell from his lips.

Stephen Corrie was one whom the world generally calls an "*excellent-hearted fellow*, an enemy to no one but himself."

We must confess that our faith in this class of excellent fellows is very small;—these men who are always sinning, and tempting others to sin, in the most amiable manner. There are few individuals who do more mischief in their day and generation than these *good-hearted* young men, these sworn enemies to temperance and morality. Like phosphoric wood, they only shine in the dark, concealing under a gay, brilliant exterior, the hollowness and corruption that festers within. Stephen Corrie was one of those men, whose heart is always proclaimed to be in the *right place*, whose bad deeds men excuse, and women adore.

The day he made his first appearance upon the deck, the captain flew into a towering passion, and marching up to him, demanded with a great oath "How the devil he came on board, and what money he had to pay his passage?"

Stephen showed his white teeth, and replied with a provoking smile—

"Not as the fair Cleopatra did to the great Cæsar, rolled up in a feather-bed; but under cover of a woman's petticoat, most noble Captain."

"Have done with your d——d fooling! Who was the bold hussy that dared to smuggle you on board?"

"I never betray a woman's secret," returned the audacious youth, bowing very low, with an air of mock gravity. "God bless the dear sex, it has befriended me ever since I could run alone! Women have been my weakness from the hour that I had discrimination enough to know the difference between a smooth cheek and a hairy one."

"And pray how do you intend to live?"

"Under the favour and patronage of the dear angels, who will never suffer their faithful slave and admirer to perish for lack of food."

"I wish them joy of their big baby," cried the rough seaman. "A most hopeful and promising child he seems by this light! And your name, sir?"

"Stephen Corrie."

"Your profession!"

"A saddler by trade, an actor by choice, a soldier by necessity. I hated the first of these, and never took well to the saddle. The second pleased me; but not my audience. And the last I took French leave of the other night, and determined to try how salt water would agree with my constitution."

"How do you think a raw hide would agree with you?" growled the Captain.

"He would be a brave fellow who would attempt to administer it," said Stephen, with a flashing eye. "But to tell you the truth, I had too much of it at home in the shop. It was my father's receipt for every sin of the flesh, and the free administration of this devilish weapon made me what I am. But softly, Captain. It is of no use putting yourself into a passion. You can't throw me overboard, and you may make me useful, since Providence has placed me here."

"Confound your impudence!" roared out old Boreas, in his stentorian voice. "Do you think that Providence cares for such a young scamp as you?"

"Doubtless, with reference to my improvement. And, as I was going to say, Captain, I am willing to work for my lodging. The women will never let such a pretty fellow as me starve; and the ship is not so crowded but that you may allow me house-room. Reach here your fist, old Nor'-wester, and say 'tis a bargain."

The Captain remained with his hands firmly thrust into his breeches' pockets; but Flora knew by the comical smile on his face that he was relenting.

"You can't help yourself, Captain, so we had better he friends."

"And you have no money?"

"Not a sixpence."

"Nor clothes?"

"None but of nature's tanning. I did not choose to walk off with the king's coat on my back; and these duds were lent me by a friend. You see, Captain, I am entirely dependent upon your bounty. You can't have the heart to be less generous than a parcel of silly women."

"You may well say, 'silly women.' But, how the deuce did you escape my observation?"

"Ah, Captain, that was easy enough. I had only to keep on the blind side."

Boreas winced—he didn't half like the joke. "Well, sir, keep on the blind side of me still. Don't let me find you cutting up any capers among the women, or by Jove you'll have to swim some dark night to Quebec without the help of a lanthorn."

"Thank you, Captain; I'll take your advice, and keep in the dark. If you want security for my good conduct, all the women in the steerage will go bail for me."

"Pretty bail, indeed! They first cheat me out of my just dues, by smuggling you on board, and then promise to give security for your good conduct. But I'll take the change out of you, never fear." And away walked the Captain, secretly laughing in his sleeve at his odd customer, who became as great a favourite with the blunt sailor as he was with his female friends.

"The fellow's not a sneak, Mrs. Lyndsay; I like him for that. And if the women choose to feed him at their own charges, he's welcome to what he can get. I shan't trouble my head with prying into his private affairs."

The truth of the matter was, that Corrie was desperately in love with a very pretty girl, called Margaret Williamson, who doubtless had smuggled her lover on hoard in female attire. The family of the Williamsons consisted of a father, two awkward rough lads, four grown-up daughters, and an old grandmother. Nannie and Jeannie, the elder daughters of the old man, were ugly, violent women, on the wrong side of thirty; Lizzie and Margaret were still in their teens, and were pretty, modest looking girls, the belles of the ship. The old grandmother, who was eighty years of age, was a terrible reprobate, who ruled her son and grandchildren with the might of her tongue—and a wicked, virulent tongue it was, as ever wagged in a woman's mouth. Constant was the war of words going on between Nannie and her aged relative, and each vied in out-cursing and scolding the other.

It was fearful to listen to their mutual recriminations, and the coarse abuse in which they occasionally indulged. But, violent as the younger fury was, her *respectable* granddame beat her hollow, for when her tongue failed, her hands supplied the deficiency, and she beat and buffeted the younger members of the family without mercy.

These two women were the terror of the steerage passengers, and the torment of the Captain's life, who was daily called upon to settle their disputes. The father of this precious crew was so besotted with drink, and so afraid of his mother and eldest daughter, that he generally slunk away into a corner, and left them the undisturbed possession of the field. How a decent-looking, well-educated young fellow, like Stephen Carrie, got entangled with such a low set, was a matter of surprise to the whole ship. But, desperately as they quarrelled among themselves, they always treated their handsome dependent with marked respect, and generously shared with him the best they had.

CHAPTER V
THE CAPTAIN'S PRENTICE

For the first ten days the *Anne* made a capital run, and the Captain predicted that if nothing went wrong with her, the port of Quebec would be made in a month, or five weeks at the farthest.

James Hawke had recovered his health and spirits, and before many days had elapsed, had made friends with every one in the ship, but the little brown man, who repelled all the lad's advances with the most dogged ill-humour. James had accomplished the feat of climbing to the top of the mast, greatly to his own satisfaction, and had won golden opinions from the Captain and all the sailors on board. He had examined every hole and corner in the ship; knew the names of most of the ropes and sails, and could lend a hand in adjusting them, with as much promptness and dexterity as if he had served an apprenticeship to the sea for years.

"That lad was born for a sailor!" was the Captain's constant cry. "I have no son of my own. If his parents would give him to me, I would make him a first-rate navigator."

James was flattered by the Captain's remarks; but he saw too much of his tyrannical conduct to a prentice lad on board, to wish to fill such a disagreeable post.

Benjie Monro was a tall, thin, sickly-looking lad of sixteen, the son of a poor widow in Newhaven, who had seen better days. The boy was proud and obstinate, and resisted the ill-treatment of his superior and his subordinates, with a determination of purpose that did him no good, but only increased his own misery.

The sailors, who knew that he was no favourite with the Captain, half-starved him, and played him a thousand ill-natured tricks. He was ill and unhappy, and tasked beyond his strength; and Mr. Collins, kind as he generally was to others, was cruel and overbearing to the wretched boy. Flora often saw the tears in Benjie's eyes, and she pitied him from her heart.

One morning Benjie had received orders to do something in his particular calling from the mate; but his commands were expressed in such a tyrannical manner, that he flatly refused to comply. Flinging himself down on the deck, he declared, "He would die first."

"We shall soon see who's master here," cried Mr. Collins, administering sundry savage kicks to the person of the half-clad boy, who lay as motionless before him as if he were really dead.

After diverting himself for some time in this way, and finding that it produced no more effect in making the lad stir than if he had been wasting his strength on a log, he called up the Captain.

"Dead is he?" said old Boreas. "Well, we'll soon bring him to life. Call Motion to fetch a light."

The light was brought, and applied to the toes and finger-ends of the boy, until they were severely scorched. His obstinate spirit, however, bore the torturing punishment without moving a muscle, or uttering the faintest moan.[A]

[A] This was the fact.

"By George! I believe he is gone at last, and a good riddance of a bad bargain," said the Captain. "If he had a spark of life left in him he could not stand that."

Lyndsay, who had been writing in the cabin, now came upon deck, and enquiring of the second mate what was going on, ran forward, and warmly interceded for the boy, telling the captain and mate in no measured terms what he thought of their conduct.

"You would not say a word in his behalf, Mr. Lyndsay," said Collins, "if you knew what a sulky rascal he was. Insensible as he appears, he is as wide awake at that this moment as you are."

"He is a miserable, heart-broken creature," said Lyndsay; "and if he had not been treated very badly, he would never attempt to act such a part."

"He's a sullen, ill-conditioned brute," said Boreas, "that's what he is."

"I know enough of human nature, Captain Williams, to feel certain that the treatment to which he has just been subjected, will never produce any beneficial change in his character."

"Who cares a curse about him!" cried Boreas, waxing wrath. "He may go to the devil for me! If he's dead, it's time the fishes had his ugly carcase. Wright (this was his second mate), tell the carpenter to get Monro's hammock, and sew him up, and throw him overboard."

A slight motion heaved the shirt about the breast of the unfortunate lad.

"You see he is coming to himself," said Lyndsay. "My lad, how do you feel now?"

The boy did not speak. The muscles of his mouth twitched convulsively, and large tears rolled down his cheeks.

"Captain," said Lyndsay, "do you see no wrong in treating a fellow-creature, and one, by your own account, born and brought up as well as yourself, like a slave?"

"He's such a disobedient rascal, that he deserves nothing better."

"Did you ever try *kindness*?"

The lad opened his large, sunken, heavy eyes, and looked at his protector with such a sad woe-begone expression, that it had the effect of touching the heart of Mr. Collins.

"I'm afraid," said he, in an aside to Lyndsay, "that we have not acted quite right in this matter. But he provokes one to anger by his sullenness. When I was a prentice on board the *Ariadne*, I was not treated a bit better; but I never behaved in that way."

"And did not the recollection of your own sufferings, Mr. Collins, plead somewhat in behalf of this orphan boy? His temper, naturally proud, has been soured by adverse circumstances, and driven to despair by blows and abusive language. I think I may pledge myself, that if he is used better, he will do his duty without giving you any further trouble."

"Get up, Benjie," said the Captain, "and go to your work. I will look over your conduct on Mr. Lyndsay's account. But never let me see you act in this mutinous manner again."

The boy rose from the deck, stammered out his thanks, and begging Mr. Collins to forgive his foolish conduct, limped off.

The next day the lad was reported to the Captain as seriously ill, and Mr. Collins, as he detailed his symptoms, said, "That he was sorry that he had used such violence towards him the preceding day, as the poor fellow had expressed himself very grateful for the non-execution of the Captain's threat of throwing him overboard."

"Oh," said Boreas, "that was only to frighten the chap. I am not such a Turk as all that, though Mrs. Lyndsay has looked very seriously at me ever since. Well, Collins, what had we better give the fellow?" And he started from the sea-chest on which he was sitting astride, and produced the medicine-chest.

Flora had forgotten all about the little red-haired doctor, Mac Adie, and the *rist o' persons*, till the sight of the condemned article met her eyes.

It was a large handsome mahogany case, inlaid with brass. The Captain opened it with a sort of mysterious awe, and displayed a goodly store of glass bottles and china boxes.

"The lad's in a high fever," said Collins. "You had better give him something that will cool his blood,—Epsom salts or cream of tartar."

"Perhaps a little of both?" said Boreas, looking up at his prime minister with an enquiring comical twinkle in his one eye.

"A single dose of either would do."

"Let it be salts then. Get me some hot water, and I'll mix it directly."

The bottle of salts was produced, and the Captain proceeded to weigh out a quarter of a pound of salts.

"Into how many doses do you propose to divide that quantity?" asked Flora, who was watching his proceedings with considerable interest.

"Divide?" said Boreas, emptying the salts into a small tea-cup, which he filled with boiling water; "he must take it at one gulp."

"Captain," said Flora, rising, and laying her hand on his arm, as he was leaving the cabin, "you will kill the boy!"

"Do you think that such a drop as that would hurt an infant?" said Boreas, holding out the cup. "Why, bless the woman! sailors are not like other folks; they require strong doses."

"Captain, I entreat you not to be so rash. Divide the quantity into four parts; add as much more water to each, and give it every four hours, and it will do good. But if you persist in administering it your way, it may be attended with very serious consequences."

"Fiddle-de-dee! Mrs. Lyndsay, I'm not going to make a toil of a pleasure. He has to take it, and once will do for all." And, in spite of her remonstrances, the obstinate old fellow went out to administer the terrible dose with his own hands to the patient. It operated as untowardly as Flora had predicted, and the lad came so near his death that the Captain grew alarmed. Perhaps his conscience tormented him not a little, for his previously harsh conduct had been the original cause of the lad's illness. So he gave up all faith in his own medical skill, and resigned the chest, and all its pernicious contents, into Flora's safe keeping.

The lad did ultimately recover from the effects of the Captain's doctoring, but he was unable to do much during the rest of the voyage, and crawled about the deck like a living skeleton.

If the Captain took little notice of him, he never treated him, or suffered others to treat him, with the brutality which had marked his former conduct towards him.

CHAPTER VI
THE LOST JACKET, AND OTHER MATTERS

The routine of life on board ship, especially on board such a small vessel as the brig *Anne*, was very dull and monotonous, when once out of sight of land. The weather, however, continued cloudless; and though, after the first week, the favourable wind which had wafted them so far over their watery path in safety deserted them, and never again filled their sails, or directed them in a straight course, they had no cause to complain. The captain grumbled at the prevalence of westerly winds; the mates grumbled, and the sailors grumbled at having to tack so often; yet the ship slowly and steadily continued to traverse the vast Atlantic, with the blue sky above, and the deep green sea below, both unruffled by cloud or storm. The health of both passengers and crew continued excellent; the prentice lad, Monro, and Mrs. Lyndsay's maid, Hannah, forming the only exceptions. As to the latter, Flora soon discovered that her illness was all apocryphal. She chose to lie in her berth all day, where she was fed from the cabin table, and duly dosed with brandy-and-water by the Captain, who did not attempt to conceal his partiality for this worthless woman. At night she was always well enough to get up and dance till after midnight on the deck with the passengers and sailors. Her conduct became a matter of scandal to the whole ship, and Mr. Collins complained of his brother-in-law's unprincipled behaviour in no measured terms. "But she's a bad woman, an infamous woman! Mrs. Lyndsay. You had better part with her the moment you reach land."

This Flora would gladly have done. But they had laid out so much money in her passage and outfit, that she did not like to incur such a heavy loss. She still hoped, that when removed from the bad influence of the Captain, she would behave herself with more propriety. A sad mistake; for this woman proved a world of trouble and sorrow, as she was both weak and wicked, and her conduct after they reached Canada occasioned her much anxiety and uneasiness.

Flora remonstrated with her, but she found her insolently indifferent to her orders. "She was free," she said, "from all engagement the moment she landed in Canada. She should be a lady there, as good as other folks, and she was not going to slave herself to death as a nurse girl, tramping about with a heavy child in her arms all day. Mrs. Lyndsay could not compel her to wait upon her on board ship, and she might wait upon herself for what she cared."

"But how do you expect to get your living in Canada?" replied Flora. "You must work there, or starve."

"Indeed!" said Hannah, tossing up her head. "It's not long that I shall stay in Canada . I'm going home with Captain Williams. He has promised to divorce his wife and marry me, when he gets back to Scotland."

"Marry you, and divorce his wife! the nice kind woman you saw on board the night we sailed! Can you lend a willing ear to such idle tales? He can neither divorce his wife nor marry you, poor, foolish girl—wicked, I should add, for your conduct, when your situation is taken into consideration, is an aggravation of hardened guilt."

"It's no business of yours, at any rate," sobbed Hannah, who had tears always at command. "I don't mean to lose the chance of being a lady in order to keep my word with you. You may get somebody else to wait on you and the child; I won't."

And she flounced back to her berth, and cried till the Captain went to console her.

This matter led to a serious quarrel with old Boreas. Lyndsay reproached him with tampering with his servant, and setting her against her employers, and threatened to write to Mr. Gregg and expose his conduct.

Boreas was first in a towering passion. He bullied, and swore, and cursed the impudent jade, who, he declared, was more competent to corrupt his morals than he was to corrupt hers. That she was his mistress, he did not deny; but as to the tale of divorcing his Jean for such a —— as her, none but a fool could believe it for a moment.

He promised, however, but very reluctantly, to conduct himself towards the girl properly for the future, and he remained as sulky and as rude as a bear to the Lyndsays for the rest of the voyage.

As to little Josey, she did not at all miss the attentions of her nurse. On deck she found abundance of nurses, from old Bob Motion to the stately Mr. Collins, who, when off duty, carried her about in his arms, singing sea songs or Scotch ballads. Her kindest and best friend, however, was Mr. Wright, the second mate. He had been brought up a gentleman, and had served his time as midshipman and master on board a King's ship, and had been broken for some act of insubordination, which had stopped his further promotion in that quarter. He had subsequently formed an imprudent marriage with some woman much beneath himself, and had struggled for many years with poverty, sickness, and heart-breaking cares. He had, in the course of time, buried this wife and seven children, and was now alone in the world, earning his living as the second mate of the small brig, the *Anne*.

The Captain disliked him, but said, "that he was an excellent seaman, and could be depended upon." The mate was jealous of him, and thought that the Captain preferred Wright to him, and considered him the ablest man of the two. But old Boreas only hated him for being a gentleman of superior birth and breeding to himself. In speaking of him he always added—"Ah, d——n him, he's a gentleman! and writes and speaks Dic. I hate gentlemen on board ship!"

Mr. Wright, with his silver hair and mild pale face, was a great favourite with Flora, and while he carried Josey in his arms to and fro the deck, she listened with pleasure to the sad history of his misfortunes, or to the graphic pictures he drew of the countries he had visited during a long life spent at sea. He fancied that Josey was the image of the last dear babe he lost,—his pet and darling, whom he never mentioned without emotion—his blue-eyed Bessy. She lost her mother when she was just the age of Josey, and she used to lie in his bosom of a night, with her little white arms clasped about his neck. She was the last thing left to him on earth, and he had loved her with all his heart; but God punished him for the sin of his youth by taking Bessy from him. He was alone in the world now—a grey-haired, broken-hearted old man, with nothing to live for but the daily hope that death was nearer to him than it was the day before, and that he should soon see his angel Bessy and her poor mother again.

And so he took to Josey, and used to call her Bessy, and laugh and cry over her by turns, and was never so happy as when she was in his arms, with her little fingers twined in his long grey locks. He would dance her, and hold her over the vessel's side to look at the big green waves, as they raced past the ship dashing their white foam-wreaths against her brown ribs, and Josey would regard them with a wondering wide-open glance, as if she wanted to catch them as they glided by.

"Always towards home," as Flora said, for the westerly winds still prevailed, and they made slow progress over the world of waters.

The Captain now found it necessary to restrain the great amount of cooking constantly going on at the caboose; and as a matter of prudence, to inspect the stores of provision among the steerage passengers. He found many of these running very low, and he represented to all on board the necessity of husbanding their food as much as possible, for he began to be apprehensive that the voyage would prove long and tedious, and the ship was only provided for a six weeks' voyage.

The good folks listened to him with an incredulous stare, as if such a calamity as starvation overtaking them was impossible. From that day—and they had been just three weeks out—the people were put upon short allowance of water, which was gradually diminished from day to day.

Unfortunately for the people on board, the weather was very warm, and no rain had fallen of any account since they left Scotland. Lyndsay and Flora had been greatly amused by a venture which an honest Northumbrian labourer was taking out to Canada, at which they had laughed very heartily. It was neither more nor less than nine barrels of *potatoes*, which they had told him was "*taking coals to Newcastle*." Droll as this investment of his small capital appeared, however, the hand of Providence had directed his choice. At the time when most of the food provided for the voyage was expended in the ship, the Captain was glad to purchase the labourer's venture at three dollars a bushel, and as each barrel contained four bushels of potatoes, the poor fellow made twenty-seven pounds of his few bushels of the "*soul-debasing root*," as Cobbett chose to style it. As he was a quiet, sensible fellow, this unhoped-for addition to his small means must have proved very useful in going into the woods. A young fellow from Glasgow, who carried out with him several large packets of kid gloves, was not half so fortunate for though they appeared a good speculation, they got spotted and spoiled by the sea water, and he could not have realised upon them the original cost.

Among the steerage passengers there was a little tailor, and two brothers who followed the trade of the awl, who always afforded much mirth to the sailors. The little tailor, who really might have passed for the ninth part of a man, he was so very small and insignificant, was the most aspiring man in the ship. Climbing seemed born in him, for it was impossible to confine him to the hold or the deck, up he most go—up to the clouds, if the mast would only have reached so high; and there he would sit or lie, with the sky above, and the sea below, as comfortable and as independent as if he were sitting crosslegged upon his board in a garret of one of the dark lofty wynds of the ancient town of Leith.

The Captain was so delighted with Sandy Rob's aspiring spirit, that he often held jocose dialogues with him from the deck.

"Hollo, Sandy! what news above there? Can't you petition the clerk of the weather to give us a fair wind?"

"Na, Captain, I'm thinkin' it's of na use until the change o' the mune. I'll keep a gude look out, an' gie ye the furst intelligence o' that event."

"And what keeps you broiling up there in the full blaze of the sun, Sandy? The women say that they are wanting you below."

"That's mair than I'm wantin' o' them. My pleasure's above—theirs is a' below. I'm jist thinkin', it's better to be here basking in the broad sunshine, than deefened wi' a' their clavers; breathin' the caller air, than suffocated wi' the stench o' that pit o' iniquity, the hould. An' as to wha' I'm doin' up here, I'm jest lookin' out to get the furst glint o' the blessed green earth."

"You'll be tanned as black as a nigger, Sandy, before you see the hill-tops again. If we go on at this rate, the summer will slip past us altogether."

Often during the night he would cry out, "Ho, Sandy! are you up there, man? What of the night, watchman—what of the night?"

"Steady, Captain—steady. No land yet in sight."

And Boreas would answer with a loud guffaw, "If we were in the British Channel, tailor, I'd be bound that you'd keep a good look-out for the Needle's eye."

The shoemakers, in disposition and appearance, were quite the reverse of the little tailor. They were a pair of slow coaches, heavy lumpish men, who would as soon have attempted a ride to the moon on a broomstick, as have ventured two yards up the mast. They were indefatigable eaters and smokers, always cooking, and puffing forth smoke from their short brass-lidded pipes. They never attempted a song, still less to join in the nightly dance on deck, which the others performed with such spirit, and entered into with such a keen relish, that their limbs seemed strung upon wires. They seldom spoke, but sat upon the deck looking on with listless eyes, as the rest bounded past them, revelling in the very madness of mirth.

Geordie Muckleroy, the elder of the twain, was a stout, clumsy made man, whose head was stuck into his broad rounded shoulders, like the handle of his body which had grown so stiff from his stolid way of thinking, (if indeed he ever thought,) and his sedentary habits, that he seemed to move it with great difficulty, and, in answering a question, invariably turned his whole frame to the speaker. He had a large, flabby, putty-coloured face, deeply marked with the small pox, from which cruel, disfiguring malady he and his brother Jock seemed to have suffered in common. A pair of little black meaningless eyes looked like blots in his heavy visage; while a profusion of black, coarse hair, cut very short, stuck up on end all over his flat head, like the bristles in a scrubbing-brush. He certainly might have taken the prize for ugliness in the celebrated club which the *Spectator* has immortalized. Yet this hideous, unintellectual looking animal had a wife, a neat, sensible-looking woman, every way his superior, both in person and intelligence. She was evidently some years older than her husband, and had left a nobleman's service, in which she had been cook for a long period, to accompany Geordie as his bride across the Atlantic. Like most women, who late in life marry very young men, she regarded her mate as a most superior person, and paid him very loving attentions, which he received with the most stoical indifference, at which the rest of the males laughed, making constant fun of Geordie and his old girl. Jock was the counterpart of his brother in manners and disposition; but his head was adorned with a red scrubbing-brush, instead of a black one, and his white freckled face was half-covered with carrotty whiskers. The trio were so poor, that after having paid their passage-money, they only possessed among them a solitary sixpence.

The day after they reached the banks of Newfoundland, and the ship was going pretty smartly through the water, Geordie hung his woollen jacket over the ship's side while he performed his ablutions, and a sudden puff of wind carried it overboard.

Mrs. Lyndsay was sitting upon the deck with Josey in her arms, when she heard a plunge into the water, followed by a loud shriek, and Mrs. Muckleroy fell to the deck in a swoon.

The cry of "A man overboard !—a man overboard!" now rang through the ship. Every one present sprang to their feet, and rushed to the side of the vessel, looking about in all directions, to see the missing individual rise to the surface of the water, and Flora among the rest.

Presently a black head emerged from the waves, and two hands were held up in a deplorable bewildered manner, and the great blank face looked towards the skies with a glance of astonishment, as if the owner could not yet comprehend his danger, and scarcely realized his awful situation. He looked just like a seal, or some uncouth monster of the deep, who having ventured to the surface, was confounded by looking the sun in the face, and was too much frightened to retreat.

Lyndsay, the moment he heard the man plunge into the sea, had seized a coil of rope which lay upon the deck, and running forward, hurled it with a strong arm in the direction in which Muckleroy had disappeared. Just at the critical moment when the apparition of the shoemaker rose above the waves, it fell within the length of his grasp. The poor fellow, now fully awake to the horrors of his fate, seized it with convulsive energy, and was drawn to the side of the vessel, where two sailors were already hanging in the chains, with another rope fixed with a running noose at one end, which they succeeded in throwing over his body and drawing him safely to the deck.

And then, the joy of the poor wife, who had just recovered from her swoon, at receiving her dead to life, was quite affecting, while he, regardless of her caresses, only shook his wet garments, exclaiming—"My jacket! my jacket, Nell, I have lost my jacket. What can a man do, wantin' a jacket?"

This speech was received with a general roar of laughter: the poor woman and her spouse being the only parties from whom it did not win a smile.

"Confound the idiot!" cried old Boreas; "he thinks more of his old jacket, that was not worth picking off a dunghill, than of his wife and his own safety. Why man," turning to the shoemaker, who was dripping like a water-dog, "what tempted you to jump into the sea when you could not swim a stroke?"

"My jacket," continued the son of Crispin, staring wildly at his saturated garments: "it was the only one I had. Oh, my jacket, my jacket!"

Strange that such a dull piece of still life should risk his life for a jacket—and an old one that had seen good service and was quite threadbare; but necessity replies, it was his only garment. A rich person can scarcely comprehend the magnitude of the loss of an only jacket to a poor man.

No one was more amused by the adventure of the jacket than Stephen Corrie, who wrote a comic song on the subject, which Duncan the fiddler set to music, and used to sing, to the great annoyance of the hero of the tale, whenever he ventured in his shirt sleeves upon the deck.

The Duncans, for there were two of them, were both highlanders, and played with much skill on the violin. They were two fine, honest, handsome fellows, who, with their music and singing kept all the rest alive. Directly the sun set, the lively notes of their fiddles called young and old to the deck, and Scotch reels, highland flings, and sailors' hornpipes were danced till late at night—often until the broad beams of the rising sun warned the revellers that it was time to rest.

The Captain and the Lyndsays never joined the dancers; but it was a pretty sight to watch them leaping and springing, full of agility and life, beneath the clear beams of the summer moon.

The foremost in these nightly revels was a young highlander called Tam Grant, who never gave over while a female in the ship could continue on her legs. If he lacked a partner he would seize hold of the old beldame, Granny Williamson, and twist and twirl her around at top speed, never heeding the kicking, scratching, and shrieking of the withered old crone. Setting to her, and nodding at her with the tassel of the red nightcap he wore, hanging so jauntily over his left eye, that it would have made the fortune of a comic actor to imitate—he was a perfect impersonification of mischief and wild mirth.

By-and-by the old granny not only got used to his mad capers, but evidently enjoyed them; and used to challenge Tam for her partner; and if he happened to have engaged a younger and lighter pair of heels, she would retire to her den below, cursing him for a rude fellow, in no lullaby strains.

And there was big Marion, a tall, stout, yellow-haired girl, from Berwickshire, who had ventured out all alone, to cross the wide Atlantic to join her brother in the far west of Canada, who was the admiration of all the sailors on board, and the adored of the two Duncans. Yet she danced just as lightly as a cow, and shook her fat sides and jumped and bounded through the Scotch reels, much in the same fashion that they did, when,

> "She up and wolloped o'er the green,
> For brawly she could frisk it."

Marion had had many wooers since she came on board; but she laughed at all her lovers, and if they attempted to take any liberties with her, she threatened to call them out if they did not keep their distance, for she had "a lad o' her ain in Canada, an' she didna care a bodle for them an' their clavers."

Yet, in spite of her boasted constancy, it was pretty evident to Flora that Rab Duncan was fiddling his way fast into the buxom Marion's heart; and she thought it more than probable that he would succeed in persuading her to follow his fortunes instead of seeking a home with her brother and her old sweetheart in the far West.

There was one sour-looking puritanical person on board, who regarded the music and dancing with which the poor emigrants beguiled the tedium of the long voyage with silent horror. He was a minister of some dissenting church; but to which of the many he belonged Flora never felt sufficiently interested in the man to inquire. His countenance exhibited a strange mixture of morose ill-humour, shrewdness, and hypocrisy. While he considered himself a vessel of grace chosen and sanctified, he looked upon those around him as vessels of wrath only fitted for destruction. In his eyes they were already damned, and only waited for the execution of their just sentence. Whenever the dancing commenced he went below and brought up his Bible, which he spread most ostentatiously on his knees, turning up the whites of his eyes to heaven, and uttering very audible groans between the pauses in the music. What the subject of his meditations were, is best known to himself: but no one could look at his low head, sly, sinister-looking eyes and malevolent scowl, and imagine him a messenger of the glad tidings that speak of peace and good-will to man. He seemed like one who would rather call down the fire from heaven to destroy, than learn the meaning of the Christ-spoken text—"I will have mercy and not sacrifice."

Between this man and Mr. Lootie a sort of friendship had sprung up. They might constantly be seen about ten o'clock p.m. seated beneath the shade of the boat, wrangling and disputing about contested points of faith, contradicting and denouncing their respective creeds in the most unchristianlike manner, each failing to convince the other, or gain the least upon his opponent.

"That is the religion of words," said Lyndsay, one day to Flora, as they had been for some time silent listeners to one of Mr. S— —'s fierce arguments on predestination—"I wonder how that man's actions would agree with his boasted sanctity?"

"Let him alone," said Flora; "time will perhaps show. I have no faith in him."

For three weeks the *Anne* was becalmed upon the Banks. They were surrounded by a dense fog, which hid even the water from their sight, while the beams of sun and moon failed to penetrate the white vapour which closed them in on every side. It was no longer a pleasure to pace the deck in the raw damp air and drizzling rain, which tamed even the little tailor's aspiring soul, and checked the merry dancers and the voice of mirth. Flora retreated to the cabin, and read all the books in the little cupboard at her bed-head. A "Life of Charles XII. of Sweden," an odd volume of "Pamela," and three of "The Children of the Abbey" comprised the Captain's library. What could she do to while away the lagging hours? She thought, and re-thought—at length, she determined to weave some strange incidents, which chance had thrown in her way, into a story, that might divert her mind from dwelling too much upon the future, and interest her husband. So unpacking her writing-desk, she set to work; and in the next Chapter we give to our readers the tale which Flora Lyndsay wrote at sea.

CHAPTER VII
NOAH COTTON. THE WIDOW GRIMSHAWE AND HER NEIGHBOURS

On the road to — —, a small seaport town on the east coast of England, there stood in my young days an old-fashioned, high-gabled, red brick cottage. The house was divided into two tenements, the doors opening in the centre of the building. A rustic porch shaded the entrance to the left from the scorching rays of the sun, and the clouds of dust which during the summer months rose from the public road in front. Some person, whose love of nature had survived amidst the crushing cares of poverty, had twined around the rude trelliswork the deliciously fragrant branches of the brier-rose, which, during the months of June and July, loaded the air with its sweet breath.

The door to the right, although unmarked by sign or chequer-board, opened into a low hedge-tavern of very ill repute, well known through the country by the name of the "Brig's Foot," which it derived from its near proximity to the bridge that crossed the river—a slow-moving, muddy stream, whose brackish waters seemed to have fallen asleep upon their bed of fat, black ooze, while creeping onward to the sea, through a long flat expanse of dreary marshes.

The "Brig's Foot" was kept by the Widow Mason and her son, both persons of notoriously bad character. The old man had been killed a few months before in a drunken brawl with some smugglers; and his name was held in such ill odour that his ghost was reported to haunt the road leading to C— — churchyard, which formed the receptacle, but it would seem not the resting-place, of the dead.

None but persons of the very lowest description frequented the tavern. Beggars made it their headquarters; smugglers and poachers their hiding-place; and sailors, on shore for a spree, the scene of their drunken revels. The honest labourer shunned the threshold as a moral pest-house, and the tired traveller, who called there once, seldom repeated the visit. The magistrates, who ought to have put down the place as a public nuisance, winked at it as a necessary evil; the more to be tolerated, as it was half a mile beyond the precincts of the town.

Outwardly the place had some attractive features, it was kept so scrupulously clean. The walls were so white, the floor so neatly sanded, and the pewter pots glittered so cheerily on the polished oak-table which served for a bar, that a casual observer might reasonably have expected very comfortable and respectable accommodation from a scene which, though on an humble scale, promised so fair. Even the sleek, well-fed tabby-cat purred so peacefully on the door-sill that she seemed to invite the pedestrian to shelter and repose.

Martha Mason, the mistress of the house, was a bad woman, in the fullest sense of the word. Cunning, hard-hearted, and avaricious, without pity, and without remorse; a creature so hardened in the ways of sin, that conscience had long ceased to offer the least resistance to the perpetration of crime. Unfeminine in mind and person, you could scarcely persuade yourself that the coarse, harsh features, and bristling hair about the upper lip, belonged to a female, had not the untamed tongue, ever active in abuse and malice, asserted its claim to the weaker sex, and rated and scolded through the long day, as none but the tongue of a bad woman can rate and scold. An accident had deprived the hideous old crone of the use of one of her legs, which she dragged after her by the help of a crutch. But though she could not move quickly in consequence of her lameness, she was an excellent hand at quickening the motions of those who had the misfortune to be under her control.

Her son Robert, who went by the familiar appellation of "Bully Bob," was the counterpart of his mother. A lazy, drunken fellow, who might be seen from morning till night lounging, with his pipe in his mouth, on the well-worn settle at the door, humming some low ribald song to chase away the lagging hours, till the shades of evening roused him from his sluggish stupor to mingle with gamblers and thieves in their low debauch. The expression of this young man's face was so bad, and his manners and language so coarse and obscene, that he was an object of dislike and dread to his low associates, who regarded him as a fit subject for the gallows. In the eyes of his mother, Bob Mason was a very fine young man—a desirable mate for any farmer's daughter in the country.

The old Spanish proverb, "Poverty makes a man acquainted with strange bedfellows," was never more fully exemplified than in the case of these people and their next door neighbours.

Dorothy Grimshawe was the widow of a fisherman, whose boat foundered in the dreadful storm of the 10th of October, 1824. Like many others, who sailed from the little port high in health and hope, expecting to reap a fine harvest from the vast shoals of herrings which annually visit that coast, Daniel Grimshawe fell a prey to the spoiler, Death, that stern fisher of men.

The following morning, after the subsidence of the gale, the beach for miles was strewn with pieces of wreck, and the bodies of forty drowned men were cast ashore! Most of these proved to be natives of the town; and the bodies being carried to the town-hall, notice was sent to the wives of the absent fishermen to come and claim their dead.

This awful summons quickly collected a crowd to the spot. Many anxious women and children were there, and Dorothy Grimshawe and her little ones came with the rest.

"Thank the good God! my man is not there," said a poor woman, coming out with her apron to her face. "The Lord save us! 'tis a fearsome sight."

"He may be food for the crabs at the bottom of the sea," said a hoarse voice from the crowd; "you are not going to flatter yourself, Nancy, that you are better off than the rest."

"Oh, oh, oh!" shrieked the poor woman, thus deprived by envy of the anchor of hope to which she clung. "I trusted in the mercy of God; I could not look to the bottom of the salt deep."

"Trust to Him yet, Nancy, and all will be well," said an old weather-beaten tar. "It is He who rules the winds and waves, and brings the storm-tossed ship into a safe harbour."

"But what has He done for these poor men? Were they worse than the rest?" sobbed Nancy.

"It is not for us to bring to the light what He has left in darkness," said the old sailor. "He took three fine lads of mine in one night, and left me childless. But it is not for the like o' me to murmur against *Him*. I always trusted to His providence, and I found that it gave me strength in the hour of danger."

"Dorothy," cried he, turning to Mrs. Grimshawe, "it is your turn to go in. It's no use crying and hanging back. Mayhap Dan has escaped the storm, an' is spreading a white sheet to the fine, fresh breeze this morning."

"My heart feels as cold as a stone," sobbed Dorothy: "I dare not go forward; I feel—I know that he is there."

"Shall I go for you? I have known Dan from a boy."

"Oh, no, no; I must see with my own eyes," said Dorothy; "nothing else will convince me that he is either saved, or lost;" and she hurried into the hall.

Trembling with apprehension, the poor woman entered the melancholy place of death. The bodies were arranged in rows along the floor, and covered decently with coarse clean sheets. The mournful and mysterious silence which always broods above the dead, was broken by sighs and sobs. Wives, mothers, sisters, and little children, were collected in heartrending groups around some uncovered and dearly-loved face, whose glassy eyes, staring and motionless, were alike unconscious of their presence and their tears.

Mrs. Grimshawe recoiled with a sudden backward step—"What if Dan is here?" She pressed her hands tightly upon her breast—the stifled cry of agony and fear that burst from her lips, nearly choked her—she clutched at the bare walls for support, and panted and gasped for breath.

A little humpbacked child, after casting upon her mother a look of unutterable pity, slowly advanced to the first shrouded figure, and, kneeling down, reverentially lifted the sheet, and gazed long and sadly upon the object beneath. "Father!" murmured the child; no other word escaped her quivering lips. She meekly laid her head upon the dead seaman's breast, and kissed his cold lips and brow with devoted affection. Then, rising from her knees, she went to her pale, weeping, distressed mother, and, taking her gently by the hand, led her up to the object of her search.

The winds and waves are sad disfigurers; but Mrs. Grimshawe instantly recognised, in the distorted features, so marred in their conflict with the elements, the husband of her youth, the father of her orphan children; and, with a loud shriek, she fell upon the bosom of the dead. Rough, pitiful hands lifted her up, and unclasped the rigid fingers that tightened about his neck, and bore the widow tenderly back to her desolate home.

Weeks went by, and the fisherman slept in his peaceful grave. His little children had ceased to weep and ask for their father, before Dorothy Grimshawe awoke to a consciousness of her terrible loss and altered fortunes. During the period of her mental derangement, her wants had been supplied by some charitable ladies in the neighbourhood. Shortly after her restoration to reason, a further trial awaited her—she became the victim of palsy. In the meridian of life she found her physical strength prostrate, and her body a useless broken machine, no longer responsive to the guidance, or obedient to the will of its possessor. An active mind shut up in a dead body,—an imprisoned bird, vainly beating itself against the walls of its cage. Human nature could scarcely furnish a more melancholy spectacle; speech, sight, and hearing, were still hers; but the means of locomotion were lost to her for ever.

The full extent of her calamity did not strike her at first. Hope whispered that the loss of the use of her lower limbs was only temporary, brought on by the anguish of her mind; that time, and the doctor's medicines, would restore her to health and usefulness.

Alas! poor Dorothy. How long did you cling to these vain hopes! How reluctantly did you at last admit that your case was hopeless,—that death could alone release you from a state of helpless suffering! Then came terrible thoughts of the workhouse for yourself and your children; and the drop was ever upon your cheek—the sigh rising constantly to your lips. Be patient, poor afflicted one! God has smitten, but not forsaken you. Pity still lives in the human heart, and help is nearer than you think.

In her early life Dorothy had lived for several years nursery-maid in a clergyman's family. One of the children entrusted to her care had loved her very sincerely; he was now a wealthy merchant in the town. When Mr. Rollins heard of her distress, he hastened to comfort and console her. He gave her part of the red-brick cottage rent free for the rest of her life; sent her two youngest daughters to school, and settled a small annuity upon her, which, though inadequate to the wants of one so perfectly dependent, greatly ameliorated the woes of her condition. Dorothy had resided several years in the cottage, before the Masons came to live under the same roof. They soon showed what manner of people they were, and annoyed the poor widow with their rude and riotous mode of life. But complaints were useless. Mr. Rollins was travelling with his bride on the Continent; and his steward, who had accepted the Masons for tenants, laughed at Dorothy's objections to their character and occupation, bluntly telling her, "that beggars could not be choosers; that she might be thankful that she had a comfortable warm roof over her head, without having to work hard for it like her neighbours." She acknowledged the truth of the remark, and endeavoured to submit to her fate with patience and resignation.

CHAPTER VIII
THE SISTERS

Mrs. Grimshawe's eldest daughter, Mary, the poor hunchback before alluded to, was a great comfort to her afflicted parent. She seldom left her bed-side, and was ever at hand to administer to her wants. Mary was a neat and rapid plain sewer; and she contributed greatly to her mother's support by the dexterity with which she plied her needle. Her deformity, which was rendered doubly conspicuous by her diminutive stature, was not the only disadvantage under which Mary Grimshawe laboured. She was afflicted with such an impediment in her speech, that it was only the members of her own family who could at all understand the meaning of the uncouth sounds in which she tried to communicate her ideas. So sensible was she of this terrible defect, and the ridicule it drew upon her from thoughtless and unfeeling people, that she seldom spoke to strangers, and was considered by many as both deaf and dumb.

Poor Mary! she was one of the meekest of God's creatures,—a most holy martyr to patience and filial love. What a warm heart—what depths of tenderness and affection dwelt in the cramped confines of that little misshapen body! Virtue in her was like a bright star seen steadily shining through the heavy clouds of a dark night. The traveller, cheered by its beams, forgot the blackness and gloom of the surrounding atmosphere.

How distinctly I can recal that plain, earnest face, after the long lapse of years! The dark, sallow cheeks; the deep, sunken, pitiful, pleading eyes; those intelligent, deep-set, iron-grey eyes, which served her for a tongue, and were far more eloquent than speech, as they gleamed from beneath her strongly-marked, jet black eyebrows; the thin lips that seldom unclosed to give utterance to what was passing in her mind, and that never smiled, yet held such a treasure of pearls within. Nature had so completely separated her from her kind, that mirth would have appeared out of place. She was plain in form and feature, but the beauty of the soul enshrined in that humble misshapen tenement, shed over her personal deformities a spiritual and holy light.

From the time of her father's death, Mary had worked steadily at her needle to support herself and the rest of the family. The constant assiduity with which she plied her task, greatly increased the projection of her shoulder, and brought on an occasional spitting of blood, which resulted from a low, hacking cough. The parish doctor who attended her bed-ridden mother, and who felt interested in her good, dutiful child, assured her that she must give up her sedentary employment, or death would quickly terminate her labour.

"But how then," asked Mary, "can I contribute to the support of the family? My mother's helpless condition requires my constant exertions. If I cease to work, she must starve."

The good doctor suggested respectable service as a more remunerative and healthier occupation.

"Alas!" said Mary, "to go into service is impossible. Who will hire a domestic who is in delicate health,—is deformed, and to strangers unintelligible? You, sir, have known me from a child. You understand my broken words. You never hurry me, so that I can make you comprehend the meaning of my jargon. But who else would have the patience to listen to my uncouth sounds?"

The doctor sighed, and said that she was right, that going out would only expose her to constant mortification and ridicule; and he felt sorry that his own means were so limited, and his family so large, that he could only afford to keep one servant, and that an active, stirring, healthy woman, able to execute, without much bodily fatigue, her multitudinous daily tasks. He left the cottage with regret; and Mary, for the first time, felt the bitter curse of hopeless poverty; and a sense of her own weakness and helplessness fell heavily on her soul.

In this emergency, Mrs. Mason offered her a trifling weekly stipend, to attend during the day upon the customers, and to assist her in washing glass and crockery, and keeping the house in order. She knew her to be honest and faithful, and she was too homely to awaken any interest in the heart of her dissipated worthless son.

Mary hesitated a long time before she accepted the offer of her repulsive neighbour; but her mother's increasing infirmities, and the severe illness of her youngest sister Charlotte, left her no choice. Day after day you might see the patient hunchback performing the menial drudgeries of the little inn, silent and self-possessed—an image of patient endurance, in a house of violence and crime. It was to her care that the house owed its appearance of neatness and outward respectability. It was her active industrious spirit that arranged and ordered its well-kept household stuff, that made the walls so cheery, the grate so gay with flowers, that kept the glittering array of pewter so bright. It was her taste that had arranged the branches of the wild rose to twine so gracefully over the rustic porch that shaded her sick mother's dwelling; who, forbidden by the nature of her disease to walk abroad, might yet see from her pillow the fragrant boughs of the brier bud and blossom, while she inhaled their fragrance in every breeze that stirred the white cotton curtains that shaded her narrow casement.

Mary's native sense of propriety was constantly shocked by unseemly sights and sounds; but their impurity served to render vice in her eyes more repulsive, and to strengthen that purity of heart from which she derived all her enjoyment. Night always released her from her laborious duties, and brought her back to be a ministering angel at the sick bed of her mother and sister.

These sisters I must now introduce to my readers, for with one of them my tale has mostly to do. Unlike Mary, they were both pretty, delicate-looking girls, ready of speech and remarkably pleasing in person and manners.

Mr. Rollins had paid for the instruction of these girls at the village school, in which they had been taught all sorts of plain work; had mastered all the difficulties of Mavor's Spelling-book, had read the Bible, the Dairyman's Daughter, Pilgrim's Progress, and Goldsmith's abridged History of England, and all the books in the shape of penny tracts and sixpenny novels they could borrow from their playmates when school was over.

Sophy, the elder of the two, who was eighteen years of age, had been apprenticed for the last two years with a milliner of an inferior grade in the little seaport town; and her term of service having expired, she had commenced making dresses in a humble way for the servants in respectable families. She had to work very hard for a very small remuneration, for the competition was very great, and without lowering her prices to nearly one-half, she could not have obtained employment at all. She could easily have procured a service as a nurse-girl or housemaid in a gentleman's family, but the novels she had read during her residence with Mrs. Makewell, the milliner, had filled her head with foolish notions of her own beauty and consequence, and given her ideas far above her humble station, quite unfitting her to submit patiently to the control of others. Besides being vain of a very lovely face, she was very fond of dress. A clever hand at her business, she contrived to give a finish and style to the homely materials she made, and which fitted so well her slender and gracefully-formed person.

Her love of admiration induced her to lay out all her scanty earnings in adorning herself, instead of reserving a portion to help to provide their daily food. Her sewing was chiefly done at home, and she attended upon her mother and sister, and prepared their frugal meals during the absence of Mary, whose situation in the "Brig's Foot" she considered a perfect degradation.

Such was Sophy Grimshawe, and there are many like her in the world. Ashamed of poverty, in which there is no real disgrace, and repining at the subordinate situation in which she found herself placed, she made no mental effort to improve her condition by frugal and patient industry, and a cheerful submission to the Divine will. She considered her lot hard, the dispensations of Providence cruel and unjust. She could not see why others should be better off than herself; that women with half her personal attractions should be permitted to ride in their carriages, while she had to wear coarse shoes and walk through the dust. She regarded every well-dressed female who passed the door with feelings of envy and hatred, which embittered her life, and formed the most painful feature in the poverty she loathed and despised.

Charlotte, the sick girl, was two years younger than Sophy, and very different in person, mind, and character. A fair, soft, delicate face, more winning than handsome, but full of gentleness and sweetness, was a perfect transcript of the pure spirit that animated the faithful heart in which it was enshrined. She might have been described in those charming lines of Wordsworth, as—

> "The sweetest flower that ever grew
> Beside a cottage door."

Contented in the midst of poverty, happy in the consciousness of moral improvement, patient under suffering, and pious without cant, or affectation of superior godliness, she offered, under the most painful circumstances, a rare example of Christian resignation to the will of God.

While reading the Gospel at school, as a portion of her daily task, it had pleased the All-Wise Dispenser of that blessed revelation to man, to open her eyes to the importance of those noble truths that were destined to set her free from the bondage of sin and death. She read, and believing that she had received a message from the skies, like the man who found the pearl of great price, she gave her whole heart and soul to God, in order to secure such an inestimable treasure. The sorrows and trials of her lowly lot were to her as stepping-stones to the heavenly land, on which all her hopes were placed, and she regarded the fatal disease which wasted her feeble frame, and which had now confined her to the same bed with her mother, as the means employed by God to release her from the sufferings of earth, and open for her the gates of heaven. How earnestly, yet how tenderly, she tried to inspire her afflicted mother with the same hopes that animated her breast! She read to her, she prayed with her, and endeavoured to explain in the best way she could that mysterious change which had been wrought in her own soul, and which now, on the near approach of death, filled her mind with inexpressible joy.

This reading of the Scriptures was a great consolation to the poor widow, and one day she remarked in a tone of deep regret and with many tears—

"Who will read the Bible to me, Charlotte, when you are gone? Mary cannot read, and if she could, who could understand what she read, and Sophy hates everything that is serious, and is too selfish to trouble herself to read aloud to me."

"Mother, I have thought much about that of late," said the sick girl, raising herself on the pillow into a sitting posture, and speaking with great earnestness. "The doctor said yesterday that I might survive for six or seven weeks longer,—'perhaps,' he added, 'until the latter end of Autumn.' During that time, could I not teach you to read?"

"At fifty years of age, Charlotte?" and the poor widow smiled at the enthusiasm of her child.

"And why not, mother?" said Charlotte, calmly. "It would be a great comfort to you, during the long, lonely hours you pass in bed; the thing may appear difficult, but I assure you that it is not impossible."

"And then your weak state; think how it would fatigue you, my dear child?"

"So far from that, mother, it would afford me the greatest delight," and the sick girl clasped her thin, wasted hands together, and looked upward with an expression of gratitude and love beaming on her pale, placid face.

"Well, I will try to please you, my dear Charlotte," said Dorothy, whose breast was thrilled to its inmost core by the affectionate solicitude which that glance of angelic benevolence conveyed to her heart; "but you will find me so stupid that you will soon give it up as a bad job."

"With God all things are possible," said Charlotte, reverentially. "With His blessing, mother, we will begin to-morrow."

It was a strange but beautiful sight[B] to see that dying girl lying in the same bed instructing her helpless mother,—a sight which drew tears from sterner eyes than mine. And virtue triumphed over obstacles which at first appeared insurmountable. Before death summoned the good daughter to a better world, she had the inexpressible joy of hearing her mother read distinctly to her Christ's Sermon on the Mount. As the old woman concluded her delightful task, the grateful Charlotte exclaimed gently, in a sort of ecstasy—"Now, Lord, let thy servant depart in peace." Her prayer was granted; and a few minutes after this good and faithful disciple entered into the joy of her Lord.

[B] This touching scene was witnessed by the Author.

This event, though long expected by Dorothy Grimshawe, was felt with keen anguish. The tuneful voice was silent, that day and night for many weeks had spoken peace to her soul. The warm young heart was still, that had so ardently hoped and prayed for her salvation, that had solved her doubts and strengthened her wavering faith, and to whom now could she turn for comfort and consolation? To Mary, whispered the voice in her soul; but Mary was absent during the greater part of the day, and Sophy was too busy with her own affairs to pay much attention to her heart-broken parent.

But deep as was the mother's grief for the loss of her dutiful child, the sorrow of the poor hunchback (for this her beloved sister, who had been the idolized pet of her joyless childhood) was greater still. Worn down with an incurable disease, Mrs. Grimshawe looked forward to a speedy reunion with the departed, but years of toil and suffering might yet be reserved for the patient creature who never was heard to murmur over her painful lot.

The death of the young Charlotte, the peacemaker, the comforter and monitor to the rest of the household, was as if her good angel had departed, and the sunshine of heaven had been dimmed by her absence.

"Oh, my sister!" she murmured in the depths of her soul, "thou wert justly dear to all; but oh! how dear to me! No one on earth loved the poor hunchback, or could read the language of her heart like you. To others dumb and uncouth, to you my voice was natural; for it spoke to you of feelings and hopes which you alone could understand."

Mrs. Mason scolded and grumbled, that, for weeks after Charlotte's death, Mary Grimshawe performed her daily tasks with less alacrity, and wandered to and fro like one in a dream. Sometimes, the pent-up anguish of her heart found a vent in sad and unintelligible sounds—"A gibberish," her mistress said, "that was enough to frighten all the customers from the house."

Mary had other causes of annoyance to grieve and perplex her, independent of the death of her sister. For some weeks past, the coarse, dissolute Robert Mason had shown a decided preference for her sister Sophy, whom he proclaimed in her hearing, to his bad associates, "to be the prettiest gal in the neighbourhood—the only gal that he cared a bit for, or deemed worth a fellow's thoughts. But then," added he carelessly, and with an air of superiority which galled Mary not a little, "the wench was poor—

too poor for him. He wanted some fun with lots of tin, that would enable him to open a good public-house in town."

Mary, as she listened, secretly blessed God that they were poor, while the ruffian continued:

"His mother, the old jade! would never consent to his marrying one so much beneath him. If she only suspected him of casting a sheep's eye at Sophy Grimshawe, she would set marks on the gal's face that would spoil her beauty. But if the gal had not been so decidedly poor, he would please himself, without asking Mammy's leave, he could tell her."

His coarse comrades received his disrespectful insubordination to his mother's authority as an excellent joke; while Mary only shuddered at his indelicate avowal of his liking for her sister, which filled her mind with a thousand indefinite fears.

Sophy, of late, had been able to obtain but little work in the neighbourhood; she was silent and dejected, and murmured constantly against her poverty, and the want of every comfort that could render life tolerable. Sometimes she talked of going into service, but, against this project, so new from her mouth, her mother objected, as she had no one else during the day to wait upon her, or speak to her. More generally, however, she speculated upon some wealthy tradesman making her his wife, and placing her at once above want and work.

"I care not," she would say, "how old or ugly he might be, if he would only take me out of this, and make a lady of me."

Mary shook her head, and tried, in hoarse ejaculations, to express her disapprobation of such an immoral avowal of sentiments she could but regard with horror; while she fixed upon her sister those piercing eyes, which seemed to look into her very soul—those eyes which, gleaming through fast-falling tears, made the vain girl shiver and turn away.

"Sophy," said Mrs. Grimshawe gravely, for the remark was made one evening, by her mother's bed-side; "Mary cannot speak her thoughts, but I understand her perfectly, and can speak them for her, and would seriously ask you, if you think it a crime to sell your soul for money?"

"Certainly not; I would do anything to get rid of the weary life I lead. All day chained down to my needle, and all night kept awake by the moans of the sick. At eighteen years of age, is it not enough to drive me mad?"

"It is what the Lord has been pleased to appoint—a heavy burden, doubtless, but meant for your good. Look at Mary: her lot is harder than yours, yet she never repines."

Sophy flashed a scornful look at her sister, as she replied—

"Mary is not exposed to the same temptations. Nature has placed her beyond them. I am handsome, and several years younger than her. She is deformed, and has a frightful impediment in her speech, and is so plain that no one could fall in love with her, or wish to make her a wife. Men think her hideous, but they do not laugh at her for being poor and shabby as they do at me."

This speech was made under the influence of vehement passion, and was concluded with a violent burst of tears.

Her cruel words inflicted a deep wound in the heart of the poor deformed girl. For the first time she felt degraded in her own eyes; and the afflictions under which she laboured seemed disgraceful; and she wished that she had been deaf as well as unintelligible. But these feelings, so foreign to her nature, were of short duration; after a brief but severe mental struggle, she surmounted her just resentment, and forgave her thoughtless sister for the unmerited reproach. Wiping the tears from her pale dark cheeks, she smoothed the pillows for her sick mother, and murmured with a sigh,—"Lord, it was Thy hand that made me as I am; let me not rebel against Thy will."

The old woman was greatly excited by Sophy's unworthy conduct. With a great effort she raised herself nearly upright in her bed, gazing sternly upon her rebellious child.

"Mary, my darling!" she cried at last, when she saw the deformed vainly striving to control the emotion which convulsed her whole frame—"bear with patience the sinful reproaches of this weak, vain girl. The time will come when she will be severely punished for her cruelty and injustice. It would be well for her if the image of her God were impressed upon her soul as it is upon yours, my good, dutiful child. The clay perishes; but that which gives value to the clay shall flourish in immortal youth and beauty when the heavens shall be no more. 'Then shall the righteous shine forth like the sun'—Ah, me! I have forgotten the rest of the text, but you, Mary, know it well; let it console you, my dear girl, and dry these useless tears. I was pretty, like Sophy, once, and, like her, I thought too highly of myself. Look at me now. Look at these wrinkled care-worn cheeks—these wasted, useless limbs; are they not a lesson to human pride and vanity? I never knew my real character until I knew grief. Sorrow has been blessed to my soul, for had I never tasted the cup of affliction, I had never known the necessity of a Saviour. May his peace and blessing fortify your heart to endure every trial which his wisdom may appoint, my poor afflicted lamb!"

Sophy's heart was softened by her mother's passionate appeal. Heartily ashamed of herself, she approached nearer to her weeping sister.

"Mary," she faltered, in a tone of deep self-reproach, "I did not mean to vex you. I know that you are better than me, and you must not take so to heart my wild words; I am miserable and unhappy; I do not always know what I say."

The eyes of the sisters met; Sophy flung her arms about Mary's neck and kissed her.

"You forgive me, Mary?"

The hunchback smiled through her tears—and such a smile, so eloquent, so full of love and grateful affection, that Sophy felt that she was more than forgiven.

"Why are you unhappy, Sophy?" asked Mrs. Grimshawe, seizing the favourable moment to make a more lasting impression on her mind.

"Because we are so poor."

"We have endured many evils worse than poverty."

"None, none. That one word comprises them all. To be hungry, shabby, despised; and you wonder that my soul rebels against it?"

"Are not unkind words and reproaches more hard to bear?"

Sophy hung her head and was silent.

"Mary would eat dry bread for a week and be cheerful and resigned, and wear a coarse, shabby garment, without shedding a single tear. These are hardships, my girl, but they do not affect the heart, or cause one pang of remorse. But, seriously, Sophy,—Do you think that you would improve your present condition, or render yourself happier, by marrying a man you did not love, for money?"

"Yes." This was said emphatically.

"Oh, do it not, my child! It is a great sin to enter into a solemn covenant, and swear at God's holy altar to love and honour and obey a man for whom you have neither affection nor respect. No blessing from God can follow such an union. Nature would assert her rights, and punish you severely for having broken her laws."

"Nonsense, mother! The thing is done every day, and I see none of these evil results. Johanna Carter married old George Hughes for his money, and they live very comfortably together. I will accept, like her, the first good offer that comes in my way."

Mary writhed, and tried for some time to make her thoughts audible: at last she succeeded in gasping out—

"Robert Mason!—not him—not him!"

"Robert Mason! What, bully Bob? Does he admire me? Well, Mary, I will quiet your apprehensions by assuring you, that the regard is not mutual. And what would the old witch his mother say?"

"Let her never have it to say, that her bad son married Daniel Grimshawe's daughter," said Dorothy, indignantly.

"Oh, but I should like to plague that old fiend, by letting her imagine that I encouraged her son. She has always something spiteful to say to me. It would be rare fun to torment her a little. I will be very sweet to Master Bob for the time to come."

Mary caught her arm, and looked imploringly in her face.

"So you are afraid of my marrying Bob Mason? What foolish women you are! He is not rich enough for me. A drunken spendthrift! When I sell my soul for money, as mother calls my getting a rich husband, it shall be to one who is better able to pay for it."

And in high spirits the hitherto discontented grumbler undressed and retired to bed, leaving Mary to pray for her during the greater part of the night, to entreat God to forgive her volatile sister, and make her sensible of her sin.

CHAPTER IX
THE GHOST

A short time after this conversation took place by the sick-bed of Dorothy Grimshawe, a report got abroad that the road between the town of ---- and C—— churchyard was haunted by the ghost of old Mason; the apparition of that worthy having been seen and spoken to by several of his old friends and associates, who had frequented the "Brig's Foot" during his occupation of it, and to whom his person was well known. The progress of the stage-coach had been several times stopped by the said ghost, the horses frightened, the vehicle overturned, and several of the passengers seriously injured. Those who retained their senses, boldly affirmed that they had seen the spectre, that it was old Mason and no mistake; a man so remarkable for his ill-looks in life, that even in death they could not be forgotten. These tales, whether true or false, were generally believed among the lower classes, and were the means of bringing a great influx of guests to the "Brig's Foot." All the idlers in the town flocked hither after the night had closed in, to ask questions, and repeat what they had heard during the day about the ghost.

Martha Mason looked sourly on her new customers, and answered all their questions regarding her departed husband with an abrupt, "What concern is it of yours what the man was like? He is dead. I know nothing about him now; nor do I want to know. I don't believe one word of your foolish lies."

One circumstance struck Mary as very singular: young Mason was always absent of an evening, and seldom returned before daybreak, particularly on those nights when the coach from N—— was expected to pass that road, which was only twice during the week. This was the more remarkable, as he had always been the foremost in the scenes of riot and misrule that were constantly enacted beneath that roof. When he did make his appearance, he was unusually sober, and repeated all the pranks performed by the ghost as an excellent joke, mimicking his looks and actions amid loud bursts of indecent laughter, to the no small horror of his superstitious guests.

"What do the ghost look like, Bob?" asked Joshua Spilman, an honest labourer, who had stepped in to drink his pint of ale, and hear the news; and having tarried later than his wont, was afraid to return home. "I never seed a ghost in all my born days."

"Why, man, ghosts, like owls, only come abroad of a night, and you have little chance of having your curiosity gratified during the day. But if you are very anxious to see one, and are not afraid of leaving the chimney-corner, and stepping out into the dark, just go with me to the mouth of the Gipsy lane, and look for yourself. It was there the old 'un appeared last night, and there most likely he'll be to-night again."

"The Lord ha' mercy upon us! Do you think, Bob, I'd put myself in the way of the ghost? I would not go there by mysel' for all the world."

"It would not hurt you."

"Not hurt I? Sure it broke the leg of Dick Simmons, when it skeared the hosses, and overturned the coach last Monday night. I'd rather keep myself in a whole skin. But when you seed it, Bob, worn't you mortal feared?"

"Not I."

"An' did you speak to 'un?"

"Ay to be sure. Do you think I'd run away from my own dad? 'Old boy,' says I, 'is that you? How are you getting on below?' He shakes his head, and glowers at me, an' his one eye looked like a burning coal.

"'You'll know one day,' says he.

"'That's pleasant news,' says I. 'You'll be sure to give me a warm welcome at any rate. There's nothing like having a friend at head quarters .' When he saw that I was not afraid of him, he gave a loud screech, and vanished, leaving behind him a most infernal stench of brimstone, which I smelt all the way from the cross-road as far as the bridge. He had got his answer; and I saw no more of him for that night."

Josh thrust his chair back to the wall, and drawing a long breath, gazed upon the reprobate with a strange mixture of awe and terror in his bewildered countenance. "Why, man, 'an my feather had said sic like words to me, I should have gone stark staring mad with fear and sheame."

"The shame should be all on his side then," quoth the incorrigible Bob. "I did not make him the bad man he was, though he made me. He was always an ugly fellow, and the scorching he has got down there (and he pointed significantly to the ground) has not improved his looks. But mother would know him in a minute."

"I never want to see your father again, Robert," said Martha, doggedly; "so you need not address any such impertinent remarks to me. I had enough of his company here. I don't know why he should leave his grave to haunt me after his death."

"For the love he bore you while on earth," said the dutiful son, glancing round the group with a knowing look. "Dad is sure of a kind reception from you, mother."

"The day he was buried," said Martha, "was the only happy one I had known for twenty years, and you know it well. One of his last acts was to make me a cripple for life."

"How did he come by his death, Mother Mason?" asked a young sailor, Tom Weston by name.

"He was killed in a row with the smugglers," said Bob. "He had helped them to land some brandy, and they wanted to cheat him out of his pay. Father had lots of pluck. He had lost an eye once before in such a frolic. He attacked the whole band single-handed, and got knocked on the head in the scuffle. The smugglers ran away, and left mother to bury the dead."

"He only got what he deserved," muttered Martha. "It is a pity he did not get it twenty years before. But he is gone to his place, and I am determined to keep mine. A ghost has no legal claim to the property of the living, and he shall never get possession of this house, living or dead, again."

"But suppose, Martha, he should take it into his head to haunt it, and make it too hot to hold you," said Tom Weston, "what would you do then?"

"I think I know a secret or two that would lay the ghost," returned Martha; and hobbling across the kitchen on her crutch, she lifted down an old horse-pistol that was suspended to one of the low cross-beams, and wiping the dust from it with her apron, she carefully examined the lock. "This should speak my welcome to all such unwelcome intruders. It has released more than one troublesome spirit from its clay tenement, and I have no doubt that it would be found equally efficacious in quieting others—that is, if they have the audacity to try their strength against me;" and she glanced disdainfully at her son from beneath her bushy lowering brows. "This brown dog is old, but he can still *bark* and *bite*!"

"How vicious mother looks!" said Bob, with a loud laugh. "It would require a ghost with some pluck to face her."

"What time did the spectre appear last night?" said Tom Weston, who saw that mischief was brewing, and was anxious to turn the subject into another channel. "I should like amazingly to see it."

"That's all bosh!" said Bob. "You would soon cut and run. But if you are in earnest, come with me to the cross-road, and I promise to introduce you to the old gentleman. The clock has just struck eleven, he will be taking his rounds by the time we get there."

The young man drew back. "Not in your company, Mason. It would be enough to raise the Devil."

"Well, please yourself. I knew you would not have pluck enough. I shall go, however. I want to have a few minutes' conversation with the ghost before he appears in public. Perhaps he will show me where to find a hidden treasure. Good-by, mother; shall I give your compliments to the old gentleman? Love, I know, is out of the question. You had none to spare for him when he was alive."

"Away with you, for a blasphemous reprobate that you are!" cried the angry old woman, shaking her crutch at him.

"Mammy's own darling son!" cried the disgusting wretch, as with a loud oath he sprang through the open door and vanished into the dark night.

The men looked significantly at each other, and a little tailor rose cautiously and shut the door.

"Why do you do that?" said Tom Weston.

"To keep out bad company."

"It is stifling hot!" cried Tom, kicking it open with his foot. "I shall die without a whiff of fresh air."

"But the ghost?" and the little tailor shook his head mysteriously.

"Does not belong to any of us," rejoined Tom. "My relations are all sound sleepers, good honest people, who are sure to rest in their graves. There is a storm brewing," he continued, walking to the open door; "that thunder-cloud will burst over our heads in a few minutes, and Master Bob will get a good drenching."

"It's awesome to hear him talk, as he do, of his feather's spirit," said honest Josh. "It makes my flesh creep upon my bones."

"Provided there's any truth in his statements," said a carpenter, who had been smoking his pipe by the table, and silently listening to the conversation,—"which I much doubt. For my own part I would be more afraid of meeting Robert Mason alone in that dark lane, than any visitant from another world. I don't believe in ghosts. I never saw one, and never met with any person on whose word you could attach much credit, that could satisfactorily prove to you that he had. When you pushed him hard, it always came out that he was not the person who had seen it; but some one else who had related the tale to him, and he had every reason to believe it true. The farther you searched into the matter, the more indistinct and improbable the story became."

"Ay, Bill Corbett; but you heard Bob declare that he has both seen and spoken to it, and the lad must know his own father."

"I don't take for gospel what I hear Bob say; I don't believe one word of the story. No, not if he were to swear to the truth of it upon the Bible," said the carpenter, waxing warm. Before Tom Weston could reply, a loud peal of thunder burst suddenly over their heads, and the room was so vividly lighted up by the electric flash which preceded it, that Mary, who was intently listening to the conversation, rose from her seat with a loud scream.

"By the living Jingo! What's that?" cried the labourer, starting to his feet, while the pipe he was smoking fell from his nerveless grasp and was shivered to atoms on the hearth.

"Pshaw!" said Tom Weston, recovering from the sudden tremor which had seized him, "'tis only the poor dummy. I thought the gal had been deaf as well as dumb."

"Why, man, the dead in their graves might have heard that!" said the terror-stricken Josh.

He had scarcely ceased speaking, when Sophy Grimshawe sprang into the room—her eyes fixed and staring, and her usually rosy cheeks livid with fear. "The thunder," she gasped, "the dreadful thunder!" and would have fallen to the ground, had not Tom Weston caught her in his arms. The unexpected sight of such a beautiful apparition, seemed to restore the young man's presence of mind. He placed her in a chair, while the little tailor bustled up to get a glass of cold water, with which he copiously bathed her face and hands. In a few minutes her limbs ceased to tremble, and opening her eyes, she glanced timidly round her. The first object that encountered her gaze, was the scornful, fiendlike face of Mrs. Mason, scowling upon her.

"So," she said sneeringly, "you make the thunder a pretext for showing your painted doll's-face to the fellows here. Your mother would do well to keep you at home."

"Mother was asleep, and she is not afraid of thunder like me. When that dreadful flash of lightning came, I dared not stay alone in the house."

"Are you a bit safer, think you, here?" sneered the witch-like woman. "It was monstrous kind of you to leave your poor old mother exposed to danger, while you run away from it like a coward! A bad excuse, however, I've heard, is better than none. In your case I think it worse."

"I did not think of that," said Sophy, with unaffected simplicity, rising to go. "Mother never cares for it, but it makes me tremble from head to foot, and almost drives me beside myself. I can't tell why, but it has always been so with me ever since I was a little child."

As she finished speaking, another long protracted peal of thunder rolled through the heavens and shook the house, and Sophy sank down gasping in her chair. The handsome young sailor was at her side with a glass of ale.

"Never mind that cross old woman, my dear, she scolds and rules us all. Take a sup of this,—it will bring the roses back to your cheeks. Why, you are as pale as the ghost we were talking of when you came in."

"Oh, I'm such a coward!" sobbed Sophy. "Ah, there it comes again—the lightning will blind me!"—and she shrieked and threw her apron over her head, as another terrific peal burst solemnly above them. "I would rather see twenty ghosts than hear the like of that again. Did not you feel the earth shake?"

"Now for the rain!" cried the little tailor, as a few heavy drops first splashed upon the door-sill, then there was the rush and roar of a hurricane, and the water burst from the skies in torrents, streaming over the door-sill and beating through the chinks in the ill-glazed windows.

"Shut the door, man! can't you?" vociferated Tom Weston to the tailor. "The rain pours in like a flood, and it will give the young lady cold."

"Poor, delicate creature," said Martha; "as if a few drops of rain could hurt the like o' her!"

As the tailor rose to shut the door, two men bearing a heavy burthen between them, filled up the before vacant space. All eyes were turned upon the strangers, as, through the howling wind and rushing rain, they bore into the room, and placed upon the back floor, a man struggling in a fit of epilepsy.

"Well, measter, how is it with 'un?" said the foremost, who was a stout rosy fellow from the labouring class.

No answer was returned to the inquiry made in a kindly tone. The person thus addressed still continued writhing in convulsions, and perfectly unconscious of his own identity or of that of any person around him.

"Put a tablespoonful of salt into his mouth, man," said Corbett the carpenter, "that will bring him to if anything will."

The simple, but powerful remedy was promptly administered by Mary, and after some minutes the paroxysms of the disorder grew less violent, and the sick man, with a heavy groan, unclosed his large dark eyes, and gazed vacantly around him,—his teeth still chattering, and his muscular limbs trembling like one in an ague fit.

"Courage, measter," said the labourer, giving him a friendly slap on the shoulder. "There's nought that can hurt thee here. See, the fire burns cheerfully, and 'tis human creturs an' friends that are about thee."

"Is it gone?" groaned the prostrate form, closing his eyes as if to shut out some frightful apparition,—"gone for ever?"

"Ay, vanished clean away into the black night."

"What did he see?" cried a chorus of eager voices; and every one in the room crowded round the fallen man.

"He seed old Mason's ghost on the bridge," said the labourer, "an' I seed it too. An ugsome looking cretur it wor, an' I wor mortal skeared, howdsomever, when measter screeched an' fell, I forgot to look on 'un agin—I wor so skeared about 'un. This good man com'd along, as luck wud ha' it, and helped me to carry 'un in here. For my part, I thought as how Measter Noah was dead; an' as he owed me four pounds and three shillings for my harvestin' with 'un, an' I had no writin' to show for it, I thought it wud be a bad job for me an' the fam'ly."

"True, neibor," said the other bearer, sententiously. "The sight of the ghost wor nothin' to that."

"And did the ghost speak to you?" said the little tailor.

"Na, na. I b'leeve that them gentry from the other world are sworn over by Satan to hold their tongues, an' never speak unless spoken to.

Howdsomever, this ghost never said a word; it stood by centre arch o' bridge, wrapped up in a winding sheet, that flickered all over like moonlight; an' it shook ter heed, an' glowered on us with two fiery eyes as big as saucers, an' then sunk down an' vanished."

"Oh, it was him—him!" again groaned forth the terror-stricken man, rising to a sitting posture. "He looked just as *he* did, that night—that night we found him murdered."

"Of whom do you speak, Master Cotton?" said the little tailor.

"Of Squire Carlos."

"Squire Carlos! Did the ghost resemble him? He has been dead long enough to sleep in peace in his grave. It is more than twenty years agone since he was murdered by that worthless scamp, Bill Martin. I was but a slip of a lad then. I walked all the way from —— to Ipswich, to see him hung. How came you to think of him?"

"It was him, or some demon in his shape," said Noah Cotton—for it was the hero of my tale—now able to rise and take the chair that the gossiping little tailor offered him. "If ever I saw Mr. Carlos in life, I saw his apparition on the bridge this night."

"A man should know his own father," mused the tailor, "and yet here is Bob Mason takes the same appearance for the ghostly resemblance of his own *respectable* progenitor. There is some strange trickery in all this. What the dickens should bring the ghost of Squire Carlos so far from his own parish? He wor shot in his own preserves by Bill Martin. I mind the circumstance quite well. A good man wor the old Squire, but over particular about his game. If I mistake not, you be Measter Noah Cotton, whose mother lived up at the porter's lodge?"

Noah nodded assent, but he didn't seem to relish these questions and reminiscences of the honest labourer, while Josh, delighted to hear his tongue run, continued—

"I kind o' 'spect you've forgotten me, Mister Cotton. I used to work in them days at Farmer Humphrey's, up Wood-lane. You have grow'd an old-looking man since I seed you last. You were young and spry enough then. I didna b'leeve the tales that volk did tell of 'un—that you were the Squire's own son. But you be as loike him now as two peas. The neebors wor right arter all."

The stranger winced, and turned pale.

"They say as how you've grow'd a rich man yoursel' since that time. Is the old 'uman, your mother, livin' still?"

"She is dead," said Noah, turning his back abruptly on the interrogator, and addressing himself to the mistress of the house. "Mrs. Mason, I have been very ill. I feel better, but the fit has left me weak and exhausted. Can you give me a bed and a room to myself, where I could sleep the effects of it quietly off?"

"My beds are engaged," was the curt reply of the surly dame. "Pray how long have you been subject to those fits?"

"For several years. Ever since I had the typhus fever. And now the least mental anxiety brings them on."

"So it appears. Particularly the sight of an old friend when least expected. This is strange," and she smiled significantly; "for he was, both living and dead, a kind friend to you."

"He was indeed," sighed the stranger. "It was not until after I lost him, that I knew how much I was indebted to him." Then suddenly turning from her, he looked stedfastly towards the open door. "It rains cats and dogs, mother; you surely cannot refuse me a bed on such a night?"

"I have already told you, I have no bed to spare. To speak the plain truth," added she, with a grim smile, "I don't like your hang-dog face, and want none of your company. If you're afraid of a shadow, you are either a great coward, or a big fool. I despise both characters. If not, you are a designing rogue, and enough of such folks come here every night."

"I will pay you well for the accommodation," urged Noah, without noticing or resenting Martha's malignant speech.

"Mother, he be as rich as a Jew," whispered Josh, in her ear.

The hint, disregarded by Mrs. Mason, was not unheeded by Sophy Grimshawe, who, gliding across the room, said, in a soft, persuasive voice: "Mr. Cotton, if you will step into the next house, I will give you my bed for the night."

"The bold hussy!" muttered Martha.

"Is it far to go?" and Noah shuddered, as he glanced into the black night.

"Only a step; just out of one door into the other. If you be afraid," she continued, looking up into his gloomy but handsome face with an arch smile, "I will protect you. I am afraid of thunder, but not of ghosts. Come along; depend upon it we shall not see anything worse than ourselves."

"There's many a true word spoken at random," said Martha, glancing after the twain, as the door closed upon them. "I'll bet all I'm worth in the world that that fellow is not afraid of nothing; he's troubled with a bad conscience. He's a hateful, unlucky-looking fellow! I'm glad that bold girl relieved me of his company."

"Martha," said Josh, "you're far wrong this time. Noah Cotton do bear an excellent character; an' then he has lots o' cash." This circumstance, apparently, gave him great importance in the poor man's eyes. "That Squire Carlos, who wor murdered by Bill Martin, left in his will a mort a' money to Noah Cotton. People do say that he wor his son."

"A likely story, that!" cried the woman, tossing up her head.

"He is very like the Squire, at any rate," said the little tailor. "I knew him for several years, and always found him a decent quiet fellow; rather proud, and fond of dressing above his rank, perhaps. But then, he always paid his tailor's bill like a gentleman. Indeed, many that I make for, who call themselves gentlemen, might take pattern by him. He was a very handsome young fellow in those days, tall, straight, and exceedingly well made; as elastic and supple as an eel; and was the best cricket-player in the county. I don't know what can have come across Noah, that he looks so gaunt and thin, and is such an old man before his time. He has been given to those terrible fits ever since he made one of the party that found the body of Mr. Carlos. It's no wonder; for he loved the Squire; and the Squire was mortal fond of him. He became very religious after he got that shock, and has been a very strict Methodist ever since."

"He's not a bit the better for that," said Martha. "The greatest sinners stand in need of the longest prayers. I thought that he had been a Methodist parson, by the cut of his jib. Where, my lads," turning to the two men who had brought him in, "did you pick the fellow up?"

"Why, do ye see, mistress, that I've been a' harvesting with 'un, an' he tuk me in the taxed cart with 'un to the bank, to get change to pay me my wages. Going into town this morning, the hoss got skeared by some boys playing at ball. The ball struck the beast plump in the eye, an' cut it so shocking bad, that measter left 'un with the hoss doctor, and proposed for us to walk home in the cool o' the evening, as the distance is only eight miles or thereabouts. Before we starts home he takes me to the Crown Inn, and treats me to a pot of ale, an' while there he meets with some old acquaintance, who was telling him how he knew his father, old Noah, in 'Mericky; an' how he had died very rich, an' left his money to a wife he had there, that he never married. An' I thought as how measter didn't much like the news, as his father, it seems, had left him nothing—not even his blessing. Well, 'twas nigh upon twelve o'clock when we started. 'You'd better stay all night, measter,' says I; ''tis nigh upon morning.' 'Sam Smith,' says he, 'I cannot sleep out o' my own bed;' and off we sets. On the bridge we heerd the first big clap o' thunder; the next minute we sor the ghost, and my measter gives a screech which might have roused old Squire Carlos from the dead, and straight fell down in a fit. The ghost vanished in the twinkling of an eye; an' I met this good man, who helped me to bring Noah up here. He's a kind measter, Noah Cotton, but a wonderful timersome man. I've heerd him, when we've been at work in the fields, start at the shivering of an aspen leaf, and cry out, 'Sam! what's that?'"

"Did not Noah say summat about having lost his yellow canvas bag with his money?" asked the other man; "and that the ghost laid hold on him with a hand as cold as ice?"

"What, did a'?" and Sam Smith opened his large, round eyes, and distended his wide, good-natured mouth, with a look of blank astonishment.

"If the ghost robbed Noah Cotton of his canvas bag, that was what no living man could do!" cried Bob Mason, bursting into the room, and cutting sundry mad capers round the floor. "Hurrah for the ghost!"

CHAPTER X
THE PROPOSAL

We will now step into the widow Grimshawe's cottage, and see how Sophy disposed of her guest.

The lower room was in profound darkness, and the little sempstress bade her companion stay at the door while she procured a light from the rush-candle, that always burnt in her mother's chamber above.

"Do not leave me in the dark!" he cried, in a voice of childish terror, and clutching at her garments. "I dare not be alone!"

"Nonsense! There are no ghosts here. I will not be gone an instant."

"Let me go with you."

"What! to my sick mother's bed-room? That cannot be. Perhaps," she continued, not a little astonished at his extreme timidity, "the ashes may still be alive in the grate. I think I perceive a faint glimmer; but you had better allow me to fetch a light from mother's room?"

"Oh no, not for the world. I beseech you to stay where you are."

Sophy knelt down by the hearth, and raking among the ashes succeeded at last in finding a live coal, which she blew into a blaze, and lighting a candle she had left on the table, placed it before him.

Her strange guest had sunk down into a large wooden arm-chair beside it, his head bent upon his clasped hands, his eyes shut, and traces of tears upon his death-pale cheeks; his lips were firmly compressed, and his countenance immovable and rigid.

Sophy gazed long and silently upon him. The sympathy of woman, be she good or bad, is always touched by the sight of a man's tears. Sophy was selfish and vain—all her faults might be comprised under those two heads; but she could not bear to witness sorrow and suffering without trying to alleviate it, unless it demanded the sacrifice of some personal gratification that she wanted strength of mind to relinquish.

The stranger had awakened her sympathy, which the knowledge that he was comparatively rich did not tend to diminish; and she examined his countenance with a degree of interest and attention which hitherto had been foreign to her nature, who had never seen anything to love or admire beyond herself.

For a person in his station, Noah Cotton was a remarkable man. His features were high and regular, his air and demeanour that of a gentleman; or rather of one who had been more used to mingle with gentlemen, than with the class to which his dress indicated him to belong. His age exceeded forty. His raven hair, that curled in close masses round his high temples, was thickly sprinkled with grey; his sallow brow deeply furrowed, but the lines were not those produced by sorrow, but care. He looked ill and unhappy, and though his dress was of the coarse manufacture generally adopted by the small yeoman or farmer, his linen was fine and scrupulously clean; in short, he was vastly superior to any of the men that frequented the "Brig's Foot."

"You are ill," said Sophy, laying her hand upon his shoulder, and speaking in a soft gentle tone. "Let me get you something to eat. I can give you some new bread, and a bowl of fresh milk."

"Thank you, my kind girl," he replied, unclosing his large, dark, melancholy eyes, and regarding her neat little figure, and fair, girlish face, with fixed attention,—"I am not hungry."

"Oh, do take a little." And Sophy placed the simple contents of the cupboard on the table before him. "It would give me real pleasure to see you eat."

"Then I will try to please you."

But, after taking a draught of the milk, Noah pushed the bowl from him, and turned gloomily to the fire, which was, now brightening into a ruddy glow, throwing cheerful red gleams to every distant corner of the room.

"And did you really see the ghost?" asked Sophy, who was dying with curiosity to hear the tale from his own mouth. And she drew a low bench beside him, and gazed earnestly up into his face. "I thought the stories about it were all humbug,—a trick played off upon the public by that worthless scamp, Bob Mason."

The man started from his abstracted fit.

"Don't speak of it now, my pretty maid. Let you and I talk of something else."

"But I should like so to know all about it. You said, when you were coming to, out of that frightful fit, that it was the ghost of a Mr. Carlos."

"Then I was a fool!" muttered Noah; but, recovering himself, he said,—"I was one of the band of men who found the body of Squire Carlos, on the night he was murdered in his own plantation, by Bill Martin, a notorious smuggler and poacher. I was very young at the time; the Squire had been a kind friend to me and my mother; and the horrid sight made such a powerful impression on my mind, that it almost deprived me of my senses, and it has haunted me ever since. I see him at all hours of the day, but most generally the vision comes before me at night, and produces these terrible fits. The doctors call it disease—I think it fate."

"How dreadful!" and Sophy recoiled involuntarily a few paces from her guest.

There was a long silence. Sophy tried to shake off the chill which had fallen upon her heart by vigorously poking the fire. At length she ventured a glance at her silent companion. He was looking down intently at her.

"You seem pretty old," she said, with that bluntness so common to uneducated people, and from which those above them wince in disgust—"are you married?"

"No, my dear; a bachelor, at your service."

"If you had a wife and children, they would cure you of these strange fancies."

"Do you really think so?"

"I am sure of it."

There was another long silence.

Her companion heaved a deep, melancholy sigh, and his thoughts seemed to break out into words, without any intention on the part of their owner.

"I have plenty to keep both wife and children, and I would gladly marry to-morrow, if I thought any good woman would have me."

Sophy smiled, and looked down into her lap. She twisted the strings of her checked apron round her fingers, the apron itself into every possible shape. At length she started from her seat.

"Where are you going?" cried the stranger, in a tone of alarm.

"To make you up a bed."

"I would rather remain by the fire all night; if you will promise to stay with me."

"But my mother would wonder what had become of me. I must leave you, and go to bed."

Noah caught her little hand as she glided past him, and pulled her violently back—

"I will not part with you—you must stay."

"Bless me, how timid you are! How you shake and tremble! I cannot understand this fear in a big man like you."

"I should grow courageous if you were always by my side."

"Perhaps you would soon be as much afraid of me as of the ghost," said Sophy, looking up into his sad eyes with a playful smile.

"The ghost again! But tell me, my pretty maid, have you a sweetheart?"

"What girl of eighteen, who is not positively ugly, has not?" returned Sophy, evasively.

"But, one whom you prefer to all others?"

"I have never yet seen that fortunate individual."

"And is there no one for whom you feel any particular liking?"

"None, I assure you."

"Good," said Noah, musingly. "Have you a father?"

"He was drowned in a heavy gale, during the fishing season, some years ago."

"A mother?"

"Yes; but she has been bed-ridden with the palsy ever since father died. Grief for his sudden loss brought it on. There are no hopes of her ever regaining the use of her limbs now."

"Any brothers or sisters?"

"One sister, the hunchbacked girl you saw in the next house; the rest are all dead. I lost a young sister about six weeks ago. She was only sixteen years of age, and as good as she was beautiful. Every body loved and respected Charlotte, and she died so happily. It was well for her. I have often envied her since she left us. I never knew what an angel she was until after we lost her."

Noah sighed again, and was silent for some minutes. At length he said,—

"Is it only good people that die in peace?"

"I don't know," said Sophy. "Charlotte was the only person I ever saw die; and her last words to us I shall never forget. 'Dear ones,' she said, while a smile from heaven rested upon her lips, 'do not weep for me. These last moments of my life are the most joyful, the happiest I have ever known. I can now fully realize that peace which our blessed Redeemer promised to all His faithful followers—a peace which surpasseth human understanding. May that His peace and blessing rest upon you all.'"

Again Noah sighed, and covered his face with his hands, and remained so long in that attitude, that Sophy imagined he had fallen asleep. At length he raised his head, and said,—

"Your father is dead, your mother infirm and old, your only sister sickly and deformed, and yourself so young and pretty, with no brothers to protect or work for you,—how do you contrive, dear girl, to maintain yourself and them?"

"Alas! we are very poor," said Sophy, bursting into tears. "I do all I can to supply the wants of the family. I have to work day and night, and Mary too, who has a cruel mistress, in order to earn our bread, yet we are often on the point of starvation; both of us are tasked beyond our strength—and I for one am heartily weary of my life."

"Dear child,"—and Noah wound his arm about her waist, and kissed away the tears from her bright blue eyes,—"if you could love and cherish an old man—old at any rate to you, although barely turned of forty, I could give both you and your afflicted mother and sister a comfortable home. I have a pleasant cottage at F——, and fifty acres of good arable land, a horse and gig, six fine milch cows, and plenty of pigs and poultry, an income of two hundred per annum in the bank, which is increasing every year, simply because I have enough to supply my household without touching either capital or interest. This property I will settle upon you, at my death, if you will become my wife."

Sophy's hand trembled in his. A bright crimson suffused her cheek, her heart leaped wildly within her breast; but she could not find a word of answer.

"I have been a bachelor all my life," continued Noah, "and a dull, cheerless life it has been to me. I had a mother to take care of in her old age, and I loved her too well to place a wife over her, who had been so long the mistress of my home. She is only lately dead, and I feel lonely and sad without her. I have often thought that I could love a wife very much. I am sure I could love you. What say you to it, my girl? Is it to be a match?"

Sophy thought of the horse and gig, and the six cows, of the pigs and poultry, of the comfortable home; and above all this, she hugged closely to her heart the 200*l.* per annum that was to be hers, besides all the rest of the worldly goods and chattels, at his death. She looked down upon her faded, shabby calico dress, and round upon the scantily furnished room, and thought of the cold, dark winter nights that were coming, and how ill-prepared they were to meet them. She remembered the days of toil, the nights of waking, watching beside the feverish bed of a querulous old woman, and she knew how fretful and impatient she was, and how her soul abhorred the task; and she turned her bright eyes to the face of her melancholy lover, and placed her small hand in his, and said in a low, soft voice, that was music to his heart,—

"I will try to love you, and will be your wife, if you will only be kind to mother and Mary, and take us from this hateful place."

Transported with joy, he promised all that she asked.

All night they sat by the fire, talking over the future prospects; and the next morning Sophia introduced Noah Cotton to her mother and sister, as her future husband, and bade them rejoice in their altered fortunes. Human nature is full of strange contradictions, and it so happened that the mother and sister did not rejoice; and instead of approving of the match, they remonstrated vehemently against it.

Sophy thought them foolish and ungrateful. She grew angry, and remained obstinately fixed to her purpose, and the affair ended in a family rupture.

Mrs. Grimshawe refused to live with Sophy, if she married Noah Cotton; and Mary could not leave her mother. Mary, who was a shrewd observer of human character, was greatly struck with the scene she had witnessed in the public house. She did not like Noah Cotton. She suspected him to be a bad man, who was labouring under the pangs of remorse rather than of disease. She had communicated these fears to her mother, and to this circumstance might be attributed her steady refusal to sanction a marriage so advantageous, in a pecuniary point of view, to them all.

Sophy was determined to secure the rich husband, and have her own way; and the very next week she became the wife of the wealthy farmer, and the newly-wedded pair left —— in a neat gig to spend the honeymoon in Noah Cotton's rural homestead in the pretty parish of F——.

CHAPTER XI
THE DISCLOSURE

Twenty months passed away, and the young bride had never once been home to visit her old friends. Her mother grew more infirm and feeble every day, and pined sadly after her absent child; and the tears were often upon Mary's cheeks. Sophy's act of wilful disobedience had been forgiven from the hour that the thoughtless rebel had become a wife; but her neglect rankled in the heart of both mother and sister.

"She has forgotten us quite," said the ailing old woman. "The distance is not great. She might come, especially as her husband keeps a horse and chaise; and what are ten miles after all? I have often walked double that in my young days to see a friend, much more a mother and sister. Well, I shall not be here long,—I feel that. The day of my release will be welcome to me, and she will be sorry when I am gone that she neglected to come and see me."

Now, though Dorothy Grimshawe, in her nervous, querulous state, grumbled over the absence of her daughter, she was never so dear to the heart of her faulty child as at the very time she complained of her neglect.

Sophy Cotton never knew the real value of a mother's love until she felt upon her own shoulders the cares and responsibilities of a house. She longed intensely to see her and Mary again, as the nice presents of butter, ham, and eggs that she was constantly sending to —— might have testified for her; but there were painful reasons that made a meeting with her mother and sister everything but desirable to the young wife.

She was changed since they parted. Her marriage had been contrary to their wishes. If she did not go over to —— in the chaise, she went nowhere else; never did the most loving bride keep more closely at home.

Once Mrs. Grimshawe asked of her daughter's messenger, a rough clodhopper, whom she had summoned to her bed-side in order to gratify her curiosity and satisfy her doubts, the reason of Mrs. Cotton's long silence—"Was she well?"

"Yes; but she had lost her rosy cheeks, and was not so blithe as when she first came to the porched-house."

"Did her husband treat her ill?"

"Na, na; he petted her like a spoilt child; yet she never seemed happy, or contented like."

"What made her unhappy then?"

"He could na just tell—women were queer creturs. Mayhap it was being an old man's wife that fretted her, and that was but natural, seeing that a pretty young thing like her might have got a husband nearer her own age, which, for sartain, would ha' been more to her taste."

"Was she likely to have any family?"

"No signs o' the like. It had na pleased the Lord to multiply Noah's seed upon the earth."

"Was he stingy?"

"Na, na; they had allers plenty to eat. He was a kind measter, an' good pay. There was only their two selves, and Mrs. Cotton was dressed like a lady, and had everything brave and new about her; but she looked mortal pale and thin, an' he b'lieved that she was in the consumption."

The man went his way, and the old woman talked to Mary about her daughter half the night. "She was always discontented with her lot," she remarked, "when single. Change of circumstances seldom changed the disposition. Perhaps it was Sophy's own fault that she was not happy."

Mary thought that her mother was right; but she felt so anxious about her sister, that she determined to leave her mother, for a few days, to the care of a kind neighbour, and walk over to F——, to ascertain how matters really stood. But her mother became seriously ill, which hindered her from putting this scheme into practice; and her uneasiness on her account banished Sophy and her affairs out of her mind.

Other events soon took place that made a material alteration in their circumstances. Mr. Rollins, their benefactor, died suddenly abroad, and, leaving no will, the pension allowed to Mrs. Grimshawe died with him. His nephew and heir had given them, through his steward, orders to quit their present abode, and poverty and the workhouse stared them in the face.

Hearing of their distress, Noah Cotton came over himself to see them, and generously offered them a home with him and his wife as long as they lived. This was done so kindly, that the sick woman forgot all her old prejudices, and she and Mary thankfully accepted his offer. But when the time came for their removal, the old woman was too ill to be taken from her bed, and the surly steward reluctantly consented that she might remain a few days longer.

Mary was anxious to leave the house. Since the appearance of old Mason's ghost, a most unpleasant notoriety was attached to it, and the most disorderly scenes were constantly being enacted beneath its roof. Persons had been robbed to a considerable amount upon the road leading to ——, which at last attracted the attention of the magistrates, and a large reward was offered for the apprehension of the person who performed the principal part in this disgraceful drama. Still, no discovery was made, until one night Bob Mason was shot by Tom Weston, who had sworn to take the ghost alive or dead. The striking resemblance this profligate young man bore to his father, had enabled him to deceive many into the belief that he was the person he represented. His mother, who was not in the secret, had never been on good terms with her son since he had personated the ghost; and the remarks he made upon his father she considered as peculiarly insulting to herself; and his dreadful end drove her mad; and this nest of iniquity was broken up. Such is the end of the wicked.

Let us now relate what had happened at the Porched House, to change the worldly Sophy Grimshawe into a pale and care-worn woman. She did not love Noah Cotton when she consented to become his wife; but he was superior to her in wealth and station, and his presence inspired her with respect and awe. He was grave and taciturn, but to her he was invariably generous and kind. Every indulgence and luxury he could afford was lavishly bestowed on his young wife; and if he did not express his attachment with the ardour of a youthful lover, he paid her a thousand little tender attentions which sufficiently proved the depth of his affection and esteem.

He was grateful to her for marrying him; and Sophy was not insensible to his efforts to render her comfortable and happy. But happy she was not, nor was ever likely to be.

Noah was a solitary man—had been so from his youth. He had been accustomed to live so many years with his old mother, and to mix so little with his neighbours, that it had made him silent and unsociable. After the first week of their marriage, he had particularly requested his young wife to try and conform to his domestic habits, and she endeavoured, for some time, to obey him. But, at her age, and with her taste for show and gaiety, it was a difficult matter; yet after awhile, she mechanically sunk into the same dull apathy, and neither went from home, nor invited a guest into the house.

Twelve months passed away in this melancholy, joyless sort of existence, when an old woman and her daughter came to reside in a cottage near them. Mrs. Martin was a kind, gossiping old body; her daughter Sarah, though some years older than Mrs. Cotton, was lively and very pretty, and gained a tolerably comfortable living for herself and her mother by dress-making. They had once or twice spoken to Sophy, on her way to the Methodist chapel, but never when her husband was present, and she was greatly taken by their manners and appearance.

"Noah, dear," she said, pressing his arm caressingly, as they were coming home one Wednesday evening from the aforesaid chapel, "may I invite Mrs. Martin and her daughter Sarah to drink tea with us? They are strangers, and it would but be kind and neighbourly to show them some little attention."

"By no means, Sophy," he cried, with a sudden start; "these people shall not enter my house."

"But why?"

"I have my reasons. They are no friends of mine. They are no strangers to me. They lived here long ago, and were forced to leave the place, after her son, a mischievous, turbulent fellow, was hung."

"Mrs. Martin's son hung!—what for? I thought they had been decent, respectable people!"

"There is no judging people by appearance," said Noah, bitterly. "I look a decent fellow, yet I have been a great sinner in my early days; and, with regard to these Martins, the less you have to do with them, Sophy, the better. I tell you, once for all, I will have no intimacy with them."

He spoke in a sterner voice than he had ever before used to his young wife. Sophy was piqued and hurt by his look and manner; and though she felt very curious to ask a thousand questions about these Martins, and on what score they had given him such offence, Noah grew so cross, and spoke so angrily, whenever she alluded to the subject, that she thought it most prudent to hold her tongue.

From the hour that these Martins came to reside at F——, Noah Cotton seemed a different creature. He was more sullen and reserved, and his attendance at the chapel was more frequent. His countenance, always pale and care-worn, now wore a troubled and anxious expression, and his athletic form wasted until he became perfectly haggard—the very spectre of his former self.

In spite of his stern prohibition, Sophy, if she did not ask the Martins to the house, often, during her husband's absence, slipped in to chat and gossip with them. Before long, her own countenance underwent a visible change, and her wasted figure and neglected dress led a stranger to suspect that she was either in a decline, or suffering from great mental depression.

Several weeks elapsed, and Mrs. Cotton had not been seen outside her dwelling by any of the neighbours. Mrs. Martin and Sarah wondered what ailed her, and both at length concluded that she must be seriously ill. But, as no doctor was seen visiting at the house, and Noah went about his farm as usual, this could hardly be the case. They were puzzled, and knew not what to think. At last, on the day that Noah went over to — —, in order to remove Mrs. Grimshawe and Mary to his own abode, the mystery was solved, and Sophy came across the road to visit her neighbours.

"Mercy, child! what aileth thee?" cried the old woman, hobbling to meet her, perfectly astonished at the melancholy alteration which a few weeks of seclusion had made in Mrs. Cotton's appearance.

"You are ill, Mrs. Cotton," said Sarah, placing the easy-chair for her guest beside the fire.

"I have not felt well for some time," returned Sophy, trying to seem composed; "and now, the alarming illness of my poor mother has quite upset me, I would have gone with Noah to — — to see her, but indeed I was not able,"—and she burst into tears.

"How long has she been sick?" asked the inquisitive old dame.

"Only a few days. Noah took the horse and cart to fetch her and Mary home to live with us. It is kind of Noah—very kind. But, God forgive me! I almost wish they mayn't come."

"Why, child, it would cheer thee up a bit. I am sure thee wantest some one to take care o' thee."

"I would rather be alone," sighed the young wife.

"What has come over thee, Sophy Cotton?" said the old woman, coming up to her and laying her hand on her shoulder, while she peered earnestly into her face. "I never saw such a cruel change in a young cretur in the course of a few weeks! But there may be a cause—a natural cause," and she smiled significantly.

"No, no, thank goodness! You are wrong—quite wrong, Mrs. Martin. No child of mine will ever sport upon my threshold, or gather daisies beside my door; and I am thankful—so thankful, that it is so!"

"That's hardly in natur'. Most o' womankind love young children—'specially their own."

"My dear Mrs. Cotton," said Sarah soothingly, "you look ill and miserable; do tell us what makes you so unhappy."

"Indeed, Sarah, I can't." And Sophy wept afresh.

"Is Noah cross to you?"

"Quite the reverse—he's the kindest of men."

"He looks very stern."

"His looks belie him."

"And do you love him?"

"If I did not, I should not be so miserable;" and Sophy laid her head down upon her knees and wept aloud.

"Mrs. Cotton, you distress us greatly," continued Sarah, taking her cold, passive hand. "Won't you tell a friend and neighbour the reason of this grief?"

But Sophy only wept as if her heart were breaking. The mother and daughter looked at each other.

The old woman returned again to the charge:—

"Tell one who loves thee like a mother."

A deep, long drawn sigh was the only answer.

"Speak out your mind, dear," said Sarah, pressing affectionately the thin, wasted hand that lay so passively within her own. "It will ease your heart."

"Ah! if I thought that you would tell no one,"—and Sophy raised her death-pale face, and fixed her earnest eyes mournfully upon her interrogator,—"I would confide to you my trouble; but oh, if you were so cruel as to betray me, it would drive me mad."

"Sure we can be trusted, Mistress Cotton," and the old woman drew herself up with an air of offended dignity. "What interest could Sarah and I have to betray thee? we be no idle gossips going clacking from house to house about matters that don't concern us. What good could it do us to blab the secrets of other folk?"

"It is only anxiety for your welfare, dear Mrs. Cotton," whispered Sarah, "that makes us wish to know what it is that troubles you."

"I believe you, my kind friends," replied Sophy. "I know I should feel better if I had the thing off my mind. It is dreadful to bear such a burthen alone."

"Does not your husband know it?"

"That is what occasions me such grief; I dare not tell him what vexes me; I once hinted at it, and I thought he would have gone mad. You wonder why I look so pale and thin; how can it be otherwise, when I never get a sound night's rest?"

"What keeps you awake?" exclaimed both women in a breath.

"My husband! He does nothing but rave all night in his sleep about some person he murdered years ago."

The women exchanged significant glances.

"Oh, if you could but hear his dreadful cries—the piteous moans he makes—the frantic prayers he puts up to God to forgive him for his great crime, and take him out of the fires of hell, it would make your hair stand on end: it makes me shiver and tremble all over with fear. And then to see, by the dim light of the rush candle, (for he never sleeps in the dark,) the big drops of sweat that stand upon his brow and trickle down his ghastly face; to hear him grind and gnash his teeth in despair, and howl in a wild sort of agony, as he strikes at the walls with his clenched fists; it would make you pray, Mrs. Martin, as I do, for the light of day. Yes, yes, it is killing me—I know it is: it is horrible to live in constant dread of the coming night—to shrink in terror from the husband in whose bosom you should rest in peace."

"Doth this happen often?" asked Mrs. Martin.

"Every night for the last two months; ever since you came to live near us. He used always to be afraid of the dark, and sometimes made a noise in his sleep, but he never acted as he does now. Once I asked him what he was dreaming about, and why he always fancied that he had murdered some one, when asleep. He flew at me like a maniac, and swore that he would throttle me if he ever heard me ask such foolish questions again; that people could not commit murder in their sleep—that they must be wide awake to shed blood."

"Ay, ay," said the old woman with a malignant smile, "doubtless he knows. Does he ever mention the name of the person he murdered, in his sleep?"

"Constantly. Did you ever, Mrs. Martin, hear of a person of the name of Carlos?"

But the old woman did not answer. A change had passed over her face, as with a cry of triumph she sprang from her seat and clapped her hands in an ecstasy of joy—it might rather be termed, of gratified revenge. "Ay! 'tis out at last! 'tis out at last! My God, I thank thee! I thank thee! Yes, yes, 'Vengeance is mine, I will repay, saith the Lord!' My Bill! my brave Bill! and thee hadst to die for this man's crime! but God has righted thee at last—at last, in spite of this villain's evidence, who swore that thy knife did the deed, when he plunged it himself into the rich man's heart. Ha, ha! I shall live to be revenged upon him—I shall, I shall!"

"What have I done!" shrieked the unhappy wife. "I have betrayed my husband into the hands of his enemies!" and she sunk down at the old woman's feet like one dead. Gloating over her anticipated revenge, Mrs. Martin spurned the prostrate form with her foot, as she scornfully commanded her more humane daughter "to see after Noah Cotton's dainty wife, while she went to the magistrates to make a deposition of what she had heard."

Shocked beyond measure at what she had heard and seen, ashamed of her mother's violence, and sorry for Sophia's unhappy disclosure, as she well knew that, whether the actual murderer of Squire Carlos, or only an accomplice, her brother was a bad man, who deserved his fate, Sarah tenderly raised the fainting Sophy from the ground, and placed her on her own bed. Long before the miserable young woman returned to a consciousness of the result of her own imprudence, her husband, who had returned from —— without her sister or mother, was on his way to the County Gaol.

CHAPTER XII
THE NIGHT ALONE

Sophy returned to her desolate home, the moment she recovered her senses; for the sight of the Martins filled her mind with inexpressible anguish. On entering the little keeping-room, she shut the door, and covering her head with her apron, sat down in Noah's chair by the old oak table, on which she buried her face in her hands, and remained silent and astonished during the rest of the day.

"Shall I sleep with you to-night, Mrs. Cotton?" said Sarah Martin, in a kind, soft voice; as towards the close of that long, blank day, she opened the door, and looked in upon

"That desolate widow—but not of the dead."

"No, Sarah, thank you; I would rather be alone," was the brief reply.

Sarah lingered with her hand still on the lock. Sophy shook her head impatiently, as much as to say, "Go, go, I must be obeyed; I know the worst now, and wish no second person to look upon my remorse—my grief—my bitter humiliation." Sarah understood it all. The door slowly closed, and Sophy was once more alone.

Many hours passed away, and the night without, dark and starless, had deepened around her cold hearth. Still Sophy sat there with her head bowed upon the table, in a sort of despairing stupor, unconscious of everything but the overwhelming sense of intense misery.

Then came painful thoughts of her past life; her frequent quarrels with her good sisters; her unkindness and neglect to her suffering mother; her ingratitude to God; and the discontented repinings over her humble lot, which had led to her present situation. She had sold herself for money; and the wealth she had so criminally coveted, was the price of blood, and from its envied possession no real enjoyment had flowed. The poverty and discomfort of her mother's cottage were small, when compared to the heart-crushing misery she at that moment endured.

Then she thought of her husband; thought of her selfish imprudence in betraying his guilt—that in his approaching trial she must appear as a principal witness against him; and that her testimony would, in all probability, consign him to the scaffold.

She felt that, however great the magnitude of his crime, he had bitterly repented of it long ago; that he had suffered untold agonies of remorse and contrition; that his punishment had been more than his reason could well bear; that he had suffered more from the pangs of conscience than he ever could experience from the hands of man. All his kindness to her, since the day she became his wife, returned to her with a sense of tenderness she never had felt for him before. She never suspected how deeply she loved him, till she was forced to part from him for ever: her soul melted within her, and she shed floods of tears.

She saw him alone in the dark dungeon, surrounded by the frightful phantoms of a guilty conscience, with no pitying voice to soothe his overwhelming grief, or speak words of peace or comfort to his tortured spirit, and she thought, "I will go to him to-morrow; I will at least say to him, I pity you, my dear unhappy husband. I pray you to forgive me for the great evil I have brought upon you."

With this thought uppermost in her mind, the miserable Sophy, overcome by her long fast, and worn out by the excitement of the past day, fell into a profound sleep.

And lo, in the black darkness of that dreary room, she thought she beheld a bright shining light. It spread and brightened, and flowed all around her like the purest moonlight, and the centre condensed into a female form, smiling and beautiful, which advancing, laid a soft hand upon her head, and whispered in tones of ineffable sweetness,—

"Pray—pray for *him* and thyself, and thou shalt find peace." The face and the voice were those of her dead sister Charlotte, and a sudden joy shot into her heart, and the vision faded away, and she awoke, and behold it was a dream.

Sophy rose up, and sank down upon the ground, and buried her face in her hands, and tried to pray, for the first time in her life, earnestly and truthfully, in the firm belief that He to whom she addressed her petition was able to help and save her, in her hour of need. Few and imperfect were her words; but they flowed from the heart, and He who looks upon the heart, gave an answer of peace.

Memory, ever faithful in the hour of grief, supplied her with a long catalogue of the sins and follies of a misspent life. Deeply she acknowledged the vanity and nothingness of those things in which she had once felt such an eager, childish delight; and she asked forgiveness of her Maker for a thousand faults that she had never acknowledged as faults before.

The world to the prosperous has many attractions. It is their paradise—they seek for no other; and to part with its enjoyments comprises the bitterness of death. Even the poor work on, and hope for better days. It is only the wounded in spirit, and sad of heart, that reject its allurements, and turn with their whole soul to God. Out of much tribulation they are new-born to life—that better life promised to them by their Lord and Saviour.

Sophy was still upon her knees, when the grey light of a rainy October morning gradually strengthened into day. Gloomy and louring, it seemed to regard her with a cheerless scowl as, shivering with cold and excitement, she unclosed the door, and stepped forth into the moist air.

"How like my earthly destiny!" she sighed. "But there is a sun behind the dark clouds, and hope exists, even for a wretch like me."

The sound of horses' hoofs approaching rapidly struck upon her ear, and the next moment she had caught hold of the bridle of the nearest rider. They were the constables, who had conducted Noah to prison, returning to the village.

"Tell me," she cried, in a voice which much weeping had rendered hoarse, and almost inarticulate, "something about my poor husband—will he be hung?"

"Nothing more certain," replied the person thus addressed. "Small chance of escape for him. The foolish fellow has confessed all."

"Then he did really commit the murder?"

"Worse than that, Mistress, he drew his own neck out of the noose, and let another fellow suffer the death he richly deserved. By his own account, hanging is too good for such a monster. He should be burnt alive."

"May God forgive him!" exclaimed Sophy, wringing her hands. "Alas! alas! He was a kind, good man to me."

"Don't take on, my dear, after that fashion," said the other horseman, with a knowing leer. "You were no mate for a fellow like him. Young and pretty as you are, you will soon get a better husband."

Sophy turned from the speaker with a sickening feeling of disgust at him and his ribald jest, and staggered back into the house. She was not many minutes in making up her mind to go to her husband. Hastily packing up a few necessaries in a small bundle, she called the old serving-man, who had lived with her husband for many years, and bade him harness the horse, and drive her to B— —.

The journey was long and dreary, for it rained the whole day. Sophy did not care for the rain; the dulness of the day was more congenial to her present feelings: the gay beams of the sun would have seemed a mockery to her bitter sorrow.

As they passed through the village, a troop of idle boys followed them into the turnpike road, shouting at the top of their voices,—

"There goes Noah Cotton's wife!—the murderer's wife! Look how grand she be in her fine chaise!"

"Ay," responded some human fiend, through an open window, loud enough to reach the ears of the grief-stricken woman; "but pride will have a fall."

The penitent Sophy wept afresh at these insults. "Oh," she sighed, "I deserve all this. I was too proud. But they don't know how miserable I am, or they would not causelessly inflict upon me another wound."

"Doan't take on so, Missus," said the good old serving-man, who, though he had said nothing to her on the subject, felt keenly for her distress. "Surely it's no fault o' yourn. You worn't born, I guess, when Measter did this fearsome deed. I ha' lived with Noe these fourteen years, an' I never 'spected him o' the like. He's about as queat a man as ever I seed. He wor allers kind to the dumb beasts on the farm, an' you know, Missus, that's a good sign. Some men are sich tyrants, that they must vent their bad humours on suffin. If the survant doan't cotch it, why the poor dumb creturs in their power do. Now I say, Noe wor a good Measter, both to man an' beast, an' I pray they may find him innocent yet."

Sophy had no hopes on the subject. She felt in her soul that he was guilty. The loquacity of honest Ben pained her, and in order to keep him silent, she remained silent herself, until they reached the metropolitan town of the county, in which the assizes were always held, which was not until late in the evening.

She could gain no admittance within the gaol that night, and Sophy put up at a small but neat public house near at hand. From the widow who kept the house, she heard that the assizes were to be held the following week, and that there was no doubt but what the prisoner, Noah Cotton, would be found guilty of murder. But her son, who was the gaoler, thought it more than probable that he would cheat the hangman, as he had scarcely tasted food since he had been in prison. Mrs. Cotton then informed the widow that she was the wife of the prisoner, and confided to her enough of her history to create for her a strong interest in the breast of the good woman. She did not fail to convey the same feeling with regard to Sophia to her son, who promised her an early interview with her husband on the following morning, and to do all for her and him that lay in his power.

Cheered with this promise, the weary traveller retired to her chamber, and slept soundly. Before six o'clock in the morning, she found herself in the presence of her husband.

CHAPTER XIII
THE MEETING

"My husband! my dear husband! and it was my imprudence that brought you to this!" cried Sophy, as she fell weeping upon the neck of the felon, clasping him in her arms, and kissing with passionate grief the tears from his haggard unshaven face.

"Hush! my precious lamb," he replied, folding her in his embrace. "It was not you who betrayed me, it was the voice of God speaking through a guilty conscience. I am thankful!—oh, so thankful that it has taken place—that the dreadful secret is known at last! I enjoyed last night the first quiet sleep I have known for years—slept without being haunted by him!"

"And with death staring you in the face, Noah?"

"What is death, Sophy, to the agonies I have endured?—the fear of detection by day—the eyes of the dead glaring upon me all night? No; I feel happy, in comparison, now. I have humbled myself to the dust—have wept and prayed for pardon, and oh, my sweet wife, I trust I am forgiven—have found peace!"

"When was this?" whispered Sophy.

"The night before last."

"How strange!" murmured Sophy. "We were together in spirit that night. I never knew how dear you were to me, Noah, until that night. How painful it would be to me to part with you for ever!"

"It was cruel and selfish in me, Sophy, to join your fate to mine,—a monster, stained with the blackest crimes. But I thought myself secure from detection; thought that my sin would never find me out, that I had managed matters with such incomparable skill that discovery was impossible, that the wide earth did not contain a witness of my guilt. Fool that I was! The voice of blood never sleeps; from out the silent dust it calls night and day in its ceaseless appeals for vengeance at the throne of God. I have heard it in the still dark night, and above the roar of the crowd in the swarming streets of London at noon-day; and ever felt a shadowy hand upon my throat, and a cry in my ear—*Thou art the man*!

"There were moments when, goaded to madness by that voice, I felt inclined to give myself up to justice, but pride withheld me, and the dismal fear of those haunting fiends chasing me through eternity, was a hell I dared not encounter. My soul was parched with an unquenchable fire; I was too hardened to pray."

"Noah," said Sophy, looking earnestly into his hollow eyes, "you are not a cruel man; you were kind to your old mother—have been very kind to me. How came *you* to commit such a dreadful crime?"

The man groaned heavily, as he replied—

"It was pride,—a foolish, false shame of low birth and honest poverty, that led me to the desperate act."

"I have felt something of this," said Sophy, and her tears flowed afresh. "I now see that sinful thoughts are but the seeds of sinful deeds, ripened and matured by bad passions. Perhaps I only needed a stronger temptation to be guilty of crimes as great as that of which you stand charged."

"Sophy," said her husband, solemnly, "I wish my fate to serve as a warning to others. Listen to me. In the long winter evenings after my mother died, I wrote a history of my life. I did this in fear and trembling, lest any human eye should catch me at my task, and learn my secret. But now that I am called upon to answer for my crime, I wish to make this sad history beneficial to my fellow-creatures.

"After I am gone, dear Sophy, and you return to F——, lose no time in taking to your home, and making comfortable, your poor afflicted mother and sister for the remainder of their days. This key" (and he drew one from his pocket) "opens the old-fashioned bureau in our sleeping-room. In the drawer nearest to the window you will find my will, in which I have settled upon you all that I possess. I have no relations who can dispute with you the legal right to this property. There is a slight indenture in the wood that forms the bottom of this drawer; press it hard with your thumb, and draw it back at the same time, and it will disclose an inner place of concealment, in which you will find a roll of Bank of England notes, to the amount of 500*l.* This was the money stolen from Mr. Carlos, the night I murdered him. It is stained with his blood, and I have never looked at it or touched it since I placed it there—upwards of twenty years ago. I never had the heart to use it, and I wish it to be returned to the family.

"In this drawer you will likewise find the papers containing an account of the circumstances which led to the commission of the crime. You and Mary can read them together; and oh! as you read, pity and pray for the unhappy murderer."

He stopped, and wiped the drops of perspiration from his brow; and the distress of his young wife almost equalled his own, as she kissed away the tears that streamed down his pale face. His breath came in quick, convulsive sobs, and he trembled in every limb.

"I feel ill," he said, in a faint voice; "these recollections make me so. There is a strange fluttering at my heart, as if a bird beat its wings within my breast. Sophy, my wife—my blessed wife! can this be death?"

Sophy screamed with terror, as he reeled suddenly forward, and fell to the ground at her feet. Her cries brought the gaoler to her assistance. They raised the felon, and laid him on his bed; but life was extinct. The agitation of his mind had been too great for his exhausted frame. The criminal had died self-condemned, under the arrows of remorse!

CHAPTER XIV
THE MURDERER'S MANUSCRIPT

Who am I, that I should write a book?—a nameless, miserable and guilty man. It is because these facts stare me in the face, and the recollection of my past deeds goads me to madness, that I would fain unburthen my conscience by writing this record of myself.

I do not know what parish in England had the discredit of being my native place. I can just remember, in the far-off days of my early childhood, coming with my mother to live at F——, a pretty rural village in the fine agricultural county of S——. My mother was called Mrs. Cotton, and was reputed to be a widow, and I was her only child. Whether she had ever been married, the gossips of the place considered very doubtful. At that period of my life this important fact was a matter to me of perfect indifference.

I was a strong, active, healthy boy, quite able to take my own part, and defend my own rights, against any lad of my own age who dared to ask impertinent questions.

The great man of the village—Squire Carlos, as he was called—lived in a grand hall, surrounded by a stately park, about a mile from F——, on the main road leading to London. His plantations and game preserves extended for many miles along the public thoroughfare, and my mother kept the first porter's-lodge nearest the village.

The Squire had been married, but his wife had been dead for some years. He was a tall, handsome man in middle life, and bore the character of having been a very gay man in his youth. It was whispered among the aforesaid village gossips, that these indiscretions had shortened the days of his lady, who loved him passionately; at any rate, she died in consumption before she had completed her twenty-fourth year, without leaving an heir to the estate, and the Squire never married again.

Mr. Carlos often came to the lodge,—so often, that he seldom passed through the gate on his way to and from the Hall without stepping in to chat with my mother. This was when he was alone; accompanied by strangers he took no notice of us at all. My mother generally sent me to open the gate. The gentlemen used to call me a pretty curly-headed boy, and I got a great deal of small change from them on hunting-days. I remember one afternoon, when opening the gate for a large party of gentlemen, with the Squire at their head, that one of them tapped my cheek with his riding whip, and exclaimed—

"By Jove! Carlos, that's a handsome boy."

"Oh, yes," said another; "the very picture of his father."

And the Squire laughed, and they all laughed; and when I went back into the lodge I showed my mother a handful of silver I had been given, and said—

"Mother, who was my father?"

"Mr. Cotton, of course," she answered gravely. "But why, Noah, do you ask?"

"Because I want to know something about him."

But my mother did not choose to answer impertinent questions; and, though greatly addicted to telling long stories, she seemed to know very little about the private memoirs of Mr. Cotton. She informed me, however, that he had been a fellow-servant with her in the Squire's employ; that he quarrelled with her shortly after I was born, and left her, and she did not know what had become of him, but she believed he went to America, and from his long silence, she concluded that he had been dead for some years. That out of respect for his services, Mr. Carlos had placed her in her present comfortable situation, and that I must show my gratitude to Mr. Carlos for all he had done for us, by the most dutiful and obliging behaviour. I likewise learned from her, that I was called Noah after my father.

This brief sketch of our family history was perfectly satisfactory to me at that time. I remember feeling a strong interest in my unknown progenitor, and used to build castles and speculate about his fate.

In the meanwhile, I found it good policy strictly to obey my mother's injunctions, and the alacrity which I displayed in waiting upon the Squire and his guests, never failed to secure a harvest of small coin, which gave me no small importance in the eyes of the lads in the village, who waited upon me with the same diligence that I did upon the Squire, in order no doubt to come in for a share of the spoil. Thus a love of acquiring without labour, and of obtaining admirers without any merit of my own, was early fostered in my heart, which led to a taste for fine dress and a boastful display of superiority, by no means consistent with my low birth and humble means.

In due time I was placed by Mr. Carlos at the village school, and the wish to be thought the first scholar in the school, and excel all my companions, stimulated me to learn with a diligence and determination of purpose, which soon placed me at the top of my class.

There was only one boy in the school who dared to dispute my supremacy, and he had by nature what I acquired with great toil and difficulty, a most retentive memory, which enabled him to repeat after once reading, a task which took me several days of hard study to learn. How I envied him this faculty, which I justly considered possessed no real merit in itself, but was a natural gift! It was not learning with him, it was mere reading. He would just throw a glance over the book, after idling half his time in play; and then walk up to the master, and say it off without making a single blunder. He was the most careless, reckless boy in the school, and certainly the cleverest. I hated him. I could not bear that he should equal, and even surpass me, when he took no pains to learn.

If the master had done him common justice, I should never have stood above him. But for some reason, best known to himself, he always favoured me, and snubbed Bill Martin, who in return played him a thousand impish tricks, and taught the other boys to rebel against his authority. Bill called me the *obsneakious* young gentleman, and Mr. Bullen, the master, the Squire's Toady.

There was constant war between this lad and me. We were pretty equally matched in strength; for the victor of to-day, was sure to be beaten on the morrow. The boys generally took part with Martin. Such characters are always popular, and he had many admirers in the school. My aversion to this boy made me restless and unhappy. I really longed to do him some injury. Once, after I had given him a sound drubbing, he called me "a base-born puppy! a beggar, eating the crumbs which fell from the rich man's table."

Foaming with rage, for a wound to my pride was far worse in my estimation, than any personal injury, I demanded what he meant by such insulting language, and he sneered in my face, and told me to go home and ask my *virtuous* mother, as she doubtless was better qualified to give me the information I desired. And I did ask my mother, and she told me "I was a foolish boy to heed such nonsense, spoken in anger by a lad I had just thrashed; that Bill Martin was a bad fellow, and envious of my being better off than himself; that if I listened to such senseless lies about her, it would make her miserable, and I should never know a happy hour myself."

I felt that this was true. I loved my mother better than anything in the world. Her affection and kindness to me was boundless. She always welcomed me home with a smiling face, and I never received a blow from her hand in my life.

My mother was about six-and-thirty years of age. She must have been beautiful in youth, for she was still very pretty. Her countenance was mild and gentle, and she was scrupulously neat and clean. I was proud of my mother. I saw no woman in her rank that could be compared with her; and any insult offered to her I resented with my whole heart and strength. I was too young to ask of her an explanation of the frequency of the Squire's visits to our house; and why, when he came, I was generally despatched on some errand to the village; and had the real explanation been given, I should not have believed it.

Mr. Carlos had no family, but his nephew and niece came twice a-year to spend their holidays at the old hall. Master Walter, who was his heir, was a fine manly fellow, about my own age, and Miss Ella, who was two years younger, was a sweet, fair girl, as beautiful as she was amiable.

I had just completed my fourteenth year, and was tall and stout for my age. Whenever these young people were at the hall, I was dressed in my best clothes, and went up every day to wait upon them. If they went fishing, I carried their basket and rods, baited their hooks, and found out the best places for their sport,—and managed the light row boat if they wished to extend their rambles further down the river.

Often we left boat and tackle, and had a scamper through the groves and meadows. I found Miss Ella birds' nests and wild strawberries, and we used to laugh and chat over our adventures on terms of perfect equality; making a feast of our berries and telling fairy tales and ghost stories. Not unfrequently we frightened ourselves with these wild legends, and ran back to the boat, and the bright river, and the gay sunshine, as if the evil spirits we had conjured up were actually before us, and preparing to chase us through the dark wood. And then, when we gained the boat, we would stop and pant, and laugh at our own fears.

Walter Carlos was a capital shot, and very fond of all kinds of field-sports. His skill with a gun made me very ambitious to excel as a sportsman. Mr. Carlos was very particular about his game. He kept several gamekeepers, and was very severe in punishing all poachers who dared to trespass on his guarded rights;—yet, when his nephew expressed a wish that I might accompany him in his favourite diversion, to my utter astonishment and delight, he took out a licence for me, and presented me with a handsome fowling-piece, which I received on my birthday from his own hand.

"This, Noah," he said, "you may consider in the way of business, as it is my intention to bring you up for a gamekeeper."

Oh, what a proud day that was to me! With what delight I handled my newly-acquired treasure! How earnestly I listened to Joe, the head gamekeeper's, directions about the proper use of it! How I bragged and boasted to my village associates of the game that *I and Master Walter* had bagged in those sacred preserves that they dared not enter, for fear of those mysterious objects of terror—man-traps and spring guns!

"The Guy! he thinks that no one can shoot but himself," sneered Bill Martin, as he turned to a train of blackguards who were lounging with him against the pales of the porter's lodge, as I, returned one evening to my mother's with my gun over my shoulder and a hare and a brace of pheasants in my hand. "I guess there be others who can shoot hares and pheasants, without the Squire's leave, as well as he. He fancies himself quite a gemman, with that fine gun over his shoulder, and the Squire's licence in his pocket."

These insulting remarks stirred up the evil passions in my breast. My gun was unloaded, but I pointed it at my tormentor, and told him to be quiet, or I'd shoot him like a dog. "Shoot and be — — to you!" says he, "it's a better death than the gallows, and that's what you'll come to."

This speech was followed by a roar of coarse laughter from his companions.

"I shall live to see you hung first!" I cried, lowering the gun, while a sort of prophetic vision of the far-off future swam before my sight. "The company you keep, and the bad language you use, are certain indications of the road on which you are travelling. I have too much self-respect, to associate with a blackguard like you."

"Dirty pride and self-conceit, should be the words you ought to use," quoth the impudent fellow. "My comrades are poor, but they arn't base-born sneaks like you."

With one blow I levelled him to the ground. Just at that moment the Squire rode up and prevented further mischief. That Bill Martin was born to be my evil genius. I wished him dead a hundred times a day, and the thought familiarized my mind to the deed. He was the haunting fiend, ever at my side to tempt me to commit sin.

CHAPTER XV
MY FIRST LOVE

Mere boy as I was, my heart had been deeply moved by the beauty of Miss Ella Carlos, I often waited upon her all day without feeling the least fatigue; and at night my dreams were full of her. I don't think that she was wholly insensible to my devotion, but it seemed a matter of amusement and curiosity to her.

I remember, one day—Oh, how should I forget it, for it formed a strong link of evil in my unhappy destiny,—that I was sitting on the bank of the river, making a cross-bow for my pretty young lady out of a tough piece of ash, for she wanted to play at shooting at a mark, and she and Master Walter were sitting beside me watching the progress of my work, when the latter said—

"I wish I were two years older."

"Why do you wish that, Watty?" asked Ella.

"Because papa says I am to go into the army at sixteen, and I do so long to be a soldier."

"But you might be killed."

"And I might live to be a great man like the Duke of Wellington," said he with boyish enthusiasm. "So, Madame Ella, set the one chance against the other."

"But it requires more than mere courage, Walter, to make a great man like him. I have heard papa say—and he fought under him in Spain—that it takes a century to produce a Wellington."

"I think papa did the Duke great injustice," said Walter. "There is not one of the heroes of antiquity to compare to him. Julius Cæsar was not a greater conqueror than Napoleon, and Wellington beat him. But great as the Duke is, Miss Ella, he was a boy once—a soldier of fortune, as I shall be; and who knows but that I may win as great a name?"

"It is a good thing, to have a fine conceit of one's self," said the provoking girl. "And what would you like to be, Noah?" she cried, with a playful smile, and turning her bright, blue eyes on me. "An Oliver Cromwell at least, as he was a man of the people; and you seem to have as good a headpiece as my valiant brother."

"I wish," I said with a sigh, which I could not repress, "that I were a gentleman."

"Perhaps you are as near obtaining your wish as Walter is. And why, Noah, do you wish to be a gentleman? You are much better off if you only knew it, as you are."

I shook my head.

"Come answer me, Noah, I want to know."

"Indeed, Miss Ella, I cannot."

"You can, and shall."

I looked earnestly into her beautiful face.

"Oh, Miss Ella, can you ask that?"

"Why not? Your reasons, Mr. Noah. Your reasons."

My eyes sought the ground. I felt the colour glow upon my cheeks, and I answered in a voice trembling with emotion,—"Because, if I were a gentleman, Miss Ella, I might then hope that you would love me; and that I might one day ask you for my wife."

The young thing sprang from the ground as if stung by a viper, her eyes flashing and her cheek crimson with passion. "*You* are an impertinent, vulgar fellow," she cried! "*You* dare to think of marrying a lady! *You*, who have not even fortune to atone for your plebeian name and low origin! Never presume to speak to me again!"

She swept from us in high dudgeon. Her brother laughed at what he termed a funny joke. I was silent and for ever. The subject was the most important to me in life. That flash of disdain from the proud bright eye—that haughty sarcastic curve of her beautiful young lip, had annihilated it. Yet, her words awoke a strange idea in my mind, that finally lured me onward to destruction. They led me to imagine, that the want of fortune was the only real obstacle between me and the attainment of my presumptuous hopes. That common as my name was, I only required the magic of gold to ennoble it; and proud as she was, if I were but rich, even she would condescend to listen to me and become mine.

From that hour Miss Ella walked and talked with me no more. I saw her daily at the hall, but she never cast upon me a passing glance, or if chance threw us in the same path, she always turned disdainfully away. The distance which every hour widened between us, only served to increase the passion that consumed me. I tried to feel indifferent to her scorn, in fact to hate her if I could, but my efforts in both cases proved abortive.

Shortly after this conversation, Mr. Walter joined the army, and Miss Ella accompanied her mother to France to finish her education; and I was placed under the head gamekeeper, to learn the art of detecting snares and catching poachers.

I filled the post assigned me with such credit to myself, and so completely to the satisfaction of my master, that after a few years, on the death of old Joe Hunter, I was promoted to his place, with a salary of one hundred pounds per annum—and the use of this cottage and farm rent free.

I now fancied myself an independent man; and my old longing for being a gentleman returned with double force; and though I had not seen Miss Ella for years, my boyish attachment was by no means diminished by absence. I determined to devote all my spare time in acquiring a knowledge of books. Our curate was a poor and studious man; to him I made known my craving for mental improvement; and as my means were more than adequate to my simple wants, and I never indulged in low vices, I could afford to pay him well for instructing me in the arts and sciences.

If Mr. Abel found me a willing pupil, I found in him a kind, intellectual instructor. Would to God I had made him a confidant of the state of my mind, and given him the true motives which made me so eager to improve myself. But from boyhood I was silent and reserved, and preferred keeping my thoughts and opinions to myself. I never could share the product of my brain with another; and this unsociable secretiveness, though it invested me with an outward decency of deportment, fostered a mental hypocrisy and self deception, far more destructive to true godliness than the most reckless vivacity.

Mr. Abel entertained a high respect for me—I was the model young man of the parish; and where-ever he went, he spoke in terms of approbation of my talents, my integrity, my filial duty to my mother, and the laudable efforts I was making to raise myself in society. This was all very gratifying to my vanity. I firmly believed in the verity of my own goodness, and considered the good curate only did me justice.

Our conversation often turned on religious matters, but my orthodoxy was so correct, my outward conduct so unimpeachable, that my title to piety of a superior cast made not the least item in the long catalogue of my virtues. And the heart all this time,—that veiled and guarded heart, whose motions none ever looked upon or suspected—was a blank moral desert; a spot in which every corrupt weed had ample space to spread and grow without let or hindrance.

As long as Mr. Abel remained in F——, I maintained the reputation I had acquired; and long after he left us, I was a regular church-goer, and prosecuted my studies both at home and abroad. At that time my personal appearance was greatly in my favour; and I was vain of my natural advantages. I loved to dress better, and appear as if I belonged to a higher grade than my village associates. This could not be done without involving considerable expense. I kept a handsome horse, and carried a handsome gun; and I flattered myself, that when dressed in my green velvet shooting jacket, white cords, top boots, and with my hunting cap placed jauntily on my head, I was as handsome and gentlemanly-looking a young fellow as could be found in that part of the country.

I had just completed my twenty-third year when Miss Ella made her appearance once more at the hall. She was no longer a pretty child, but had grown into a lovely and accomplished woman. A feeling of despair mingled with my admiration when she rode past me in the park, accompanied by a young gentleman and an elderly lady.

The gentleman was a younger brother, who afterwards died in India; the lady was her mother. Miss Ella was mounted on a spirited horse, which she sat to perfection, her nobly proportioned figure displayed to the best advantage by her elegant and closely fitting dark blue riding habit.

After they passed me, the elderly lady bent forward from her horse and said to her daughter, loud enough for me to hear. "Ella, who is that handsome young man?—he looks a gentleman."

"Far from that, Mamma," returned the young lady saucily. "It is my uncle's gamekeeper, Noah Cotton. The lad I once told you about. He is grown very handsome. But what a name, Noah," and she laughed—such a merry mocking laugh. "It is enough to drown any pretensions to good looks."

"How came you to know the man, Ella?" said her brother gravely.

"Oh, George, you know Uncle is not over particular. An aristocrat with regard to his game, and any infringement on his rights on that score, but a perfect democrat in his familiarity with his domestics and tenants. He used to send for this Noah to play with us during the holidays. He was a beautiful, curly-headed lad; and we treated him with too much condescension, but it was Uncle's fault;—he should have known that the boy was no companion for young people in our rank. This saucy, spoilt boy, had not only the impudence to fall in love with me, but to tell me so to my face."

"The scoundrel!" muttered the young man.

"Of course I never spoke to him again. I complained to Uncle, and he only treated it as a joke. It is a pity," she added, in a less boastful and haughty tone, "that he is not a gentleman: he is a handsome, noble-looking peasant."

They rode out of hearing, leaving me rooted to the spot. The sudden turn in the path had hidden me from their observation, and brought them and the theme of their conversation too terribly near.

Miss Ella's description of me cut into my heart, and stung me like an adder. I pressed my hand upon my burning brain,—upon my aching heart, I tried to tear her image from both. Vain effort! Passion had done its work effectually. The limning of years could not be effaced by the desecrating power of mortified vanity.

I saw her many times during that visit to the Hall; but, beyond raising my cap respectfully when she passed me, no word of recognition ever escaped from my lips. Once or twice I thought, from her manner, and the earnest way in which she regarded me, that she almost wished me to speak to her.

Her horse ran away with her one morning in the park, and she lost her seat, but received no serious injury. I caught the animal, and helped her to remount. Our eyes met, and she blushed very deeply, and her hand trembled as it lay for a moment in mine. Trifling as these circumstances were, they gave birth at the time to the most extravagant hopes, which filled me with a sort of ecstasy. I almost fancied that she loved me,—she, the proud, highborn, beautiful lady. Alas! I knew little of the coquetry of woman's nature, or that a girl of her rank and fortune would condescend to notice a poor lad like me, to gratify her own vanity and love of admiration.

I went home intoxicated with delight; and that night I dreamt I found a vast sum of gold beneath a pine-tree in one of the plantations, and that Ella Carlos had consented to become my wife. My vision of happiness was, however, doomed to fade. The next day Mrs. Carlos and her son and daughter left the Hall, and I did not see her again before she went.

For weeks after their departure I moped about in a listless, dispirited manner, loathing my menial occupation, and despising the low origin which formed an insurmountable barrier between me and the beautiful mistress of my heart.

I was soon roused from these unprofitable speculations, and called to take an active part in the common duties of my every-day life. Some desperadoes had broken into the preserves, and carried off a large quantity of game. Mr. Carlos vowed vengeance on the depredators, and reprimanded me severely for my neglect.

This galled my pride, and made me return with double diligence to my business. After watching for a few nights, I had every reason to believe that the poacher was no other than my old enemy. Bill Martin, after an absence of several years in America, had suddenly reappeared in the village, and was constantly seen at the public-house, in the company of a set of worthless, desperate characters. He had sunk into the low blackguard, and manifested his hatred to me by insulting me on all occasions. My dislike to this ruffian was too deep to find vent in words. I was always brooding over his injurious conduct, and planning schemes of vengeance.

One day, in going through the plantations, I picked up a large American bowie-knife, with Bill Martin's name engraved upon the handle. This I carefully laid by, hoping that it might prove useful on some future occasion. Meanwhile, the game was nightly thinned; and the caution and dexterity with which the poachers acted, baffled me and my colleagues in all our endeavours to surprise them in the act.

CHAPTER XVI
TEMPTATION

"That Bill Martin is a desperate ruffian," said Mr. Carlos to me one morning, after we were returning to the Hall through the park. I had been watching in the preserves all night, but nothing had transpired, beyond the discovery of the bowie-knife, that could lead to the detection of the marauders. "I have no doubt that he and his gang are the party concerned in these nightly depredations; but we want sufficient proof for their apprehension."

"Give Martin rope enough, and he'll hang himself," I replied. "He is fierce and courageous, but boastful and foolhardy. In order to astonish his companions, he'll commit some daring outrage, and betray himself. I will relax a little from our vigilance, to give him more confidence, and put him off his guard. It won't be long, depend upon it, before we have him safely lodged in ——gaol."

"Noah, my boy, you are a trump!" cried the Squire, throwing his arm familiarly across my shoulder. "It's a pity such talents as you possess should be wasted in watching hares and partridges."

I felt my heart heat, and my cheeks glow, and I thought of Miss Ella. "Was he going," I asked myself, "to place me in a more respectable situation?"

But no; the generous fit passed away, and he broke into a hearty laugh.

"D——e, Noah, I had half a mind to buy a commission for you, and make a soldier of you. But you had better remain as you are. That confounded name of Noah Cotton would spoil all. Who ever heard of a gentleman bearing such a cognomen? It is worse than Lord Byronis."

"Amas Cottle, Phœbus, what a name! What could tempt your mother to call you after the old patriarchal navigator! Ha! ha! it was a queer dodge."

"It was my father's name," said I, reddening; for, besides being bitterly mortified and disappointed, I by no means relished the joke; "and my father, though poor, was an honest man!"

"Both cases *rather* doubtful," said the Squire, laughing to himself. Then, slapping me pretty sharply on the shoulder, he said,—"And what, my lad, do you know of your father?"

"Nothing, personally; to the best of my knowledge I never saw him; but my mother has told me a good deal about him."

"Humph!" said Mr. Carlos. "Did she tell you how much she was attached to Mister Noah Cotton, and how grieved she was to part with such a tender, loving spouse?"

"Sir, Mr. Carlos,—do you mean to insult me by speaking in this jeering way of my parents?"

"Not in the least, Noah; so don't look at me with that fierce black eye, as if you took me for a hare or a pheasant, or, worse than either, for Bill Martin. *You* ought to know that I am your friend,—have been your friend from a child; and if you continue to conduct yourself as you have done, will befriend you for life."

I looked, I am sure, very foolish, for I felt his words rankling in my heart; and, though I affected to laugh, I strode on by his side in silence; the chain of obligations he had wound around me, and my dependence upon him, tightening about me, and galling me at every step. He certainly saw that I was offended, for, stopping at the gate which led from the park to the Hall-gardens, where our roads separated, he said, rather abruptly,—

"You are angry with me, Noah?"

"With you, sir?—that would be folly."

"It would, indeed. I see you can't bear a joke."

"Not very well."

"You don't take after your father, then, for he loves a joke dearly."

"Is my father alive?" I cried, eagerly.

"Of course he is."

"My mother don't know this."

"As well as I know it. Women have all their secrets. They don't tell us all they know. One of these days you'll hear more about this mysterious father, depend upon it."

I longed to ask him all he knew upon the subject, but we were not on terms of familiarity to warrant such a liberty. He was my master, and it was his part to speak—mine to listen. Presently he turned the subject into another channel altogether.

"By-the-by, Noah," said he, "I am going to-day to ——. I have a large sum of money to receive from my lawyer,—the payment for Crawford's farm, which I sold a few months ago. The land was bad, and I was offered a good price for it,—more, indeed, than I thought it was worth. Horner advised me to sell, and I sold it accordingly. It may be late when I return to-morrow night, which I shall do by the F—— coach. It will put me down on the other side of the park, and I shall have to walk home by the plantations, and through the great avenue; and, though the distance is but a mile, to tell you the truth, I should not like to meet Bill Martin and his gang, after nightfall, in such a lonely place, especially with a large sum of money on my person,—at least from 500*l.* to 1,000*l.* I wish you would bring your gun, and wait for the coming up of the coach, at the second gate, which leads into that lonely plantation. It will be in by ten o'clock."

"That I will, with the greatest pleasure," I cried, and all my petty resentment vanished. "I am not afraid of twenty Bill Martins. I only wish I may have the luck to meet with him."

"I shall feel perfectly safe with you, Noah. But—hallo! I forgot, is not to-morrow the great cricket-match at S——? and you must be there."

"It is," said I; "but there is no positive necessity for my being there. It is a good thing to be missed sometimes. They'll know the value of a good player another time."

"You are their best hand?"

"Yes; I know *that*, and they know it too. However, for this time they must try and win the match without me. Good morning, Mr. Carlos, I will not fail to meet you as you desire."

He entered the magnificent lawn which spread in front of his noble residence, and I, whistling the tune of a hunting-song, turned my steps through the plantations towards home.

God knows! at that moment I had not the most distant idea of raising my hand against his life.

I walked on, or rather sauntered, for the weather was excessively warm for September, in a sort of dreamy state. The thought uppermost in my mind was a vague wish to know how much money Mr. Carlos expected to receive for the sale of Crawford's farm.

The land was not very good; but the house and barns were commodious, and in excellent repair. It was honestly worth £4,000. Will he receive this large sum in one payment—or will it be by instalments of eight hundred or a thousand pounds? The latter supposition was the most probable. "He is foolish," I continued, pursuing my train of thought, "to travel with a sum like that in his pocket, and by a common conveyance too. It is tempting providence. But he is a rash man, who never listens to any advice. He will be murdered one of these days if he does not take care."

A thousand pounds is an immense sum in the estimation of a poor man. The busy fiend whispered in my ear, "How much could be done with that sum if you could only command it! It would buy a commission in the army, and make a gentleman of you at once." But then "people would suspect how I came by it."

"It would enable you to emigrate to America or Australia; and become the purchaser of a tract of land, that might make your fortune."

"Yes! and then I would drop the odious name of Noah Cotton, return with a fine coat, and a noble alias, and seek out and marry my adored Ella Carlos."

After indulging for some time in this species of castle-building, I began seriously to consider whether it would be such a difficult matter to obtain the money, and realize the latter of these dreams.

I did not wish to inflict any personal injury on Mr. Carlos, who had always been very kind to me and my mother; yet he was a person for whom I felt little respect, and I often reproached myself for my want of gratitude to our mutual benefactor.

He had a fine person, and a frank generous bearing, but his manners were coarse and familiar, and his language immoral, and beneath the dignity of a gentleman. I had frequently seen him intoxicated; and while in that state I had often assisted him from his carriage, and guided his tottering steps up the broad stone steps that led to his mansion.

I had often remarked to my mother, when such an event had filled me with deep disgust, "Had Mr. Carlos been a poor man, he would have been a great blackguard."

And she would grow very red and angry—more so than I thought the occasion required, and say, "My son, it is not for the like of us to censure the conduct of our betters. It is very unbecoming, especially in you, on whom the Squire has conferred so many favours. You ought to shut your eyes and ears, and tell to no one what you see and hear."

I did neither the one nor the other. I was keenly alive to the low pursuits of my superior, whom I only considered as such, as far as his rank and wealth were concerned, for hitherto I had led a more moral life than he had. I neither gambled, nor drank, nor swore; had never seduced a poor girl to her ruin, and then boasted of my guilt. If the truth must be spoken, I regarded the Squire with feelings of indifference, which amounted almost to contempt, which all sense of past obligations could not overcome.

Oh, if these spoilt children of fortune did but know the light in which such deeds are regarded by the poor, and the evils which arise from their bad example, they would either strive to deserve their respect, or at least strive to keep their immoralities out of sight!

It is, perhaps, no excuse for my crime to say, that had Mr. Carlos been a good man, I should never have been a bad one, or have been tempted under any circumstances to have taken his life; yet I do feel certain, that if that had been the case, he would have been safe, and I had never fallen. I should have tried to show my gratitude to him, by deserving his esteem; as it was, I felt that his good opinion of me was of little worth, that he could not prize good qualities in me to which he was himself a stranger. The only tie which bound me to him was one of self-interest. He paid me well, and for the sake of that pay, I had up to this period been a faithful, diligent servant.

But what has all this to do with my temptation and fall? Much, oh, how much; the conviction of the worthlessness of my master's character, and the little loss his death would be to the community at large, drowned all remorseful feelings on his behalf, and hastened me far on the road to crime.

After having once indulged the idea that I could easily rob him, and make myself master of the property he had on his person, I could not again banish it from my mind. I quickened my pace, and recommenced whistling a gay tune; but the stave suddenly ceased, and in fancy I was confronting Mr. Carlos by that lonely avenue-gate. I rubbed my eyes to shut out the horrid vision, and began slashing the thistles which grew by the roadside, with my cane. Then I thought I saw him pale, and weltering in his blood, at my feet; and I heard Bill Martin's fiendish laugh and his prophecy respecting the gallows.

I stopped in the middle of the road, and looked hard at the dust. What a terrible idea had that one thought of Bill Martin's conjured up. The opportunity to gratify my long-treasured hatred—to avenge myself on my enemy, was within my grasp!

That knife—I walked quickly on—I nearly ran, driven forward by the excitement under which I laboured. Yes—that knife, with his name upon the handle. If the deed were done adroitly, and with that knife, and I could but contrive to send him to the spot a few minutes after the murder had been committed, he would be the convicted felon, I the possessor of wealth that might ultimately pave the way to fortune.

I was now near the village, and I saw a bosom friend of Martin's, with a suspicious-looking dog lounging at his heels. I knew that anything said to Adam Hows, would be sure to be retailed to his comrades, for with Bill Martin I never held the least communication.

CHAPTER XVII
THE PLOT

"A fine day, Mister Game-keeper," quoth Adam, "prime weather for shooting. Have you much company at the Hall?"

"No one at present. The Squire expects a large party the beginning of the week."

"Is there much game this season?" asked the poacher, very *innocently*.

"There *was*," I replied, rather fiercely. "But these rascally poachers are making it scarce. I only wish I had the ringleader of the gang within the range of this gun."

"How savage you are, Cotton! A soft, easy name that for a hard, cruel fellow. Why not live and let live? What is it to you, if a poor fellow dines now and then off the leg of a hare, or the wing of a pheasant? It don't take one penny out of your pocket. What right have these rich men to lay an embargo upon the beasts of the field, and the fowls of the air? Ay, upon the very fish that swims in the stream, which God gave for the use of all. Tyrants!—they have not enough of the good things of this world, but they must rob the poor of their natural rights. I only wish I had them under the range of that, which a poor man dare not carry without a licence, in a free land. But there will come a day,"—and he ground his teeth,—"pray God that it may come soon, when these cursed game laws, and their proud makers, shall be crushed under our feet."

"That will not be in your day—nor yet in mine, Adam Hows. No, not if we both lived to the age of your venerable namesake of apple-eating celebrity. Like him—you seem to have a hankering for forbidden fruit; and taste it too, I apprehend, if I may judge by that lurcher at your heels. You are wrong to keep that dog. It has a suspicious look."

"I am not acquainted with his private tastes," said Adam, patting the snaky-headed brute. "Like his betters, he may relish a hare now and then; but I never saw him eat one. Fox, my boy! Are you fond of game?—the keeper thinks you are. Fie, fox, fie. It is as bad to look like a thief, as to be one."

"You had better put that dog away, Adam. If the Squire sees him, he will order him to be shot."

"D—— the Squire! Who cares for the Squire. He poaches on other preserves besides his own. Hey, Mister Cotton?"

The colour flushed my face—I scarce knew why. "I don't understand your joke."

"Oh, no, of course not. You are such an innocent fellow. But there are others who do. Are you going to the cricket-match to-morrow? The fellows of S—— have challenged our fellows to a grand set-to on their common: 'tis famous ground. The men of S—— play well—but our bullies can beat them. I am told that you are the flash man of the F—— club?"

"I love the sport—it is a fine manly, old English game; I should like to go very well, and they expect me; but I have an engagement elsewhere."

"You'll have to put it off."

"Impossible."

"But the honour of the club."

"Must yield to duty. I promised to meet Mr. Carlos at the second avenue gate to-morrow night, at eleven o'clock."

"D——, has he turned thief-taker? Does he mean to catch the poachers himself? Well, if that is not a queer dodge for a gentleman."

"He would not be a bad hand," said I laughing; "No, no. The coach puts him down there on his return from I——, and I promised to see him safe home."

"Safe home! Why, man, 'tis only a mile from the hall. Is he afraid of ghosts?"

"Not at all," I said, dropping my voice. "No one who knows Squire Carlos, could ever take him for a coward. But there are a great many suspicious characters in the neighbourhood, and the Squire returns with a large sum of money on his person. He was afraid that he might be robbed in that lonely place, and he asked me, as a particular favour, to meet him there with my gun."

"A large sum of money did you say?" and the poacher drew nearer and gazed upon me with an eager and excited stare. "Does he often travel abroad with such sums about him?"

"Not often. This is a particular case—it is the price of the farm he sold lately, Crawford's farm, and he wants the money to make another purchase. Perhaps he will have with him a couple of thousand pounds."

"You don't say—and you are to meet him at the second avenue gate at eleven o'clock?"

"So I promised. But don't, there's a good fellow, mention it to any one. I would not for the world be thought to blab my master's secrets. He would never forgive me, if it came to his ears. To tell you the truth, I don't much like the job. I would rather have a jolly day with the club at S— —. I am sure we should win the match."

"I thought the coach came in at ten?" said Adam, still dreaming over the vision of gold.

"Not on market-nights. It is always late. Eleven was the hour he appointed."

"Oh, of course, he knows best. And such a large sum of money! I would not venture on the road with twenty shiners in my pocket. But two thousand! The man's a fool. Good day, Noah—don't raise a bad report against my poor dog. You know the old proverb—'Give a dog a bad name.' Two thousand pounds—my eye, what a sum!"

Away trudged the poacher, with the game-destroyer at his heels. I sat down upon a stile, and looked after him. I was sure of my man.

"Go your ways to Bill Martin," said I. "Tell him the tale I have told to you, and between us, Mr. Carlos has small chance of sleeping on a feather-bed to-morrow night."

I felt certain that an attempt would be made to rob Mr. Carlos by these ruffians. I read it in the fellow's eye. "I would bet my life that neither of us go to the cricket-match to-morrow at S— —. Bill will have a different job on hand. It will be the ball and not the bat, that is to win the game they hope to play."

I had only to be at the place at the right hour, and with a dexterous blow stun, without killing my victim, and secure the prize; and then return and detect the ruffians in the very act. For this purpose, I determined to secure the cooperation of another gamekeeper, who might accompany me to the avenue, and help me to secure the villains. I was so elated with this plan, that I forgot my own share of the guilt. The leaven of iniquity that I had introduced into the breast of another, was already at work, and two human beings were subjected to the same temptation to which I had yielded.

It is astonishing how a fellowship in guilt hardens the guilty. Men, like wolves, are often great cowards alone; but give them a few companions in crime, and pusillanimity is instantly converted into ferocity. The coward is always cruel; the mean-spirited, merciless. The consciousness that two of my fellow-men premeditated committing the same crime, wonderfully strengthened me in my resolution of plunging my soul into the abyss of guilt. I had another passion to gratify, which had rankled for years in my breast,—that of revenge. A wish to over-reach and disappoint Bill Martin was a stronger incentive to this deed than the mere lucre of gain. The burning hatred I had cherished from boyhood was on the eve of being gratified. I should, in case of failure on my part, at least secure his destruction.

When I reached home, I found two of the principal members of the cricket-club, both respectable tradesmen in the village, waiting to see me. I was their best hand, and they left no argument unurged, in order to induce me to go. I took them separately aside, and confidentially informed them of my reasons for staying at home. This I justly thought would avert all suspicion from me as the real culprit. Of course they were convinced that my going was out of the question, and took their leave with regret.

My mother was not very well. She had a bad head-ache, and complained of being very nervous, (a fine word she had picked up from the parson's wife,) and we passed a very dull evening together.

I had never before shunned my mother's eye; but this night I could not look steadily at her. She at length noticed my agitation, and asked if anything had gone wrong with the game.

I said, "Nothing more than usual; that I was sorry that I could not go to the match; that I was afraid our men would be beaten without me; that I had a great mind to send the second keeper, George Norton, who was a brave, honest fellow, to meet my master, and start for S—— the next day."

"You must do no such thing," she said sharply. "You must meet Mr. Carlos, as you promised him, yourself. If any harm should happen to the Squire through your neglect, we shall lose the best friend we have in the world. You must not think of leaving him to the care of another. He will be justly displeased, and it may mar your fortune for life."

"In what way, Mother?" said I gloomily. "I think you place too much importance on the 'Squire's good-will. I could earn my own living, if I were out of employ to-morrow."

My mother replied, "that I was proud and ungrateful. That Mr. Carlos had raised me out of the dirt, and I ought to be ready to lay down my life to serve him."

I retorted. She grew angry, and for the first time in my life, she went to bed without kissing and bidding me good-night, or wishing that God might bless me.

I felt the omission keenly. It seemed as if my good angel had forsaken and left me to my fate. For a long time I sat brooding over the fire. My thoughts were full of sin. I went to the cupboard where my mother kept a few simple medicines, and a small bottle of brandy in case of accidents or sudden illness. I hated ardent spirits, and seldom took anything stronger than a cup of tea or milk; or, when very tired, a little home-brewed ale. But this night, I took a large glass of brandy—the first raw liquor I had ever drunk in my life. Stupefied and overpowered, I soon found relief from torturing thoughts, in a heavy, stupid sleep.

Breakfast was on the table when I unclosed my eyes. The remains of the brandy were replaced in the cupboard, and my poor mother was regarding me with a sad countenance and tearful eyes.

"You were ill, Noah, last night?"

"I had a confounded head-ache."

"And you did not tell me."

"You parted with me in anger, Mother. I felt so miserable! We never had a quarrel before, and I took the brandy to raise my spirits. It had a contrary effect. It made me drunk for the first time in my life."

"I hope it will be the last."

"Yes; if the repetition does not prove more agreeable. My temples throb—my limbs tremble—everything is distasteful. Who could feel pleasure in a vice so bestial?"

"Habit, Noah, reconciles us to many things which at first awaken only aversion and disgust. All pleasure which has its foundation in sin must end in pain and self-condemnation. Drunkenness is one of those vices which when first indulged creates the deepest shame and humiliation; but custom renders it a terrible necessity."

My mother could preach well against any vice to which she was not particularly inclined herself. I never saw her take a glass of wine or spirits in my life. This was from sheer want of inclination; all strong drinks were disagreeable to her taste.

I took a cup of tea, and after immersing my head in cold water, the nausea from which I was suffering gradually abated, and I soon felt well again. While I was standing at the open window I saw Adam Hows and Bill Martin pass the lodge. They were in earnest conversation. I called to Adam, and asked him, "If he were going to see the cricket-match?"

He answered, that it depended upon the loan of a horse. Harry Barber had promised them his; but it had broken pasture, and they were going in search of it.

I did not believe this statement. I was certain that it was intended for a blind. I told Adam, that in case he did not find Barber's horse, I would lend him mine. He was profuse of thanks, but did not accept my offer. He was certain of finding the lost animal in time: he was going to drive over his friend to S— —, and my mare did not go in harness. I took no notice of his companion. For many months we had never spoken to each other—not even to exchange insults. At four o'clock in the afternoon I heard that they were drinking in a low tavern just out of the village. If I did not keep my appointment with 'Squire Carlos, I felt convinced that they would.

CHAPTER XVIII
THE MURDER

All day I was restless, and unable to settle to the least thing. My mother attributed my irritation and ill-humour to the brandy I had drunk on the preceding evening. As the night drew on, I was in a perfect fever of excitement; yet not for one moment did I abandon the dreadful project. I had argued myself into the belief that it was my fate—that I was compelled by an inexorable destiny to murder Mr. Carlos. I was to meet him at ten o'clock—just one hour earlier than the time I had named to Adam Hows. At eight my mother went to bed, complaining of indisposition. I was glad of this, for it left me at perfect liberty to arrange my plans.

I dressed myself in a waggoner's frock and hat, in order to conceal my person from my victim, and with Bill Martin's bowie knife in the breast of my waistcoat and a large knotted bludgeon in my hand, almost a fac-simile of one often carried by that ruffian, I sallied into the road. My disguise was so complete, that few without a very near inspection would have detected the counterfeit. Fortunately I met no one on the road whom I knew, and reached the second gate in the dark avenue which led to the one which opened into the high road, just ten minutes before the coach drove up. I heard the bluff voice of the coachman speaking to the horses. I heard Mr. Carlos, in his frank, cheerful tones bid the coachman good-night. The stage rattled on, and the 'Squire's measured step (for he had been a soldier in his youth) sounded upon the hard gravel path that led from the avenue to the plantation-gate, by the side of which I was concealed, behind the trunk of a vast oak that cast its dense shadows across the road. Above, the moon was shining in a cloudless sky.

After the first gate which opened upon the road had swung to after him, Mr. Carlos commenced singing a favourite hunting-song, perhaps to give me warning of his approach, or to ascertain if I had been true to my word.

Nervous as I had been all day, I was now calm and collected. I had come there determined to rob him, and nothing but the certainty of detection could have induced me to abandon my purpose.

When he reached the gate, he called out in his clear voice, "Noah—Noah Cotton! are you there?"

Receiving no answer, he opened the gate, and passed through. As he turned to shut it, I sprang from my hiding-place, and with one blow successfully, but not mortally aimed, I felled him to the ground. Contrary to my calculations, he stood erect for a moment, and instead of falling forward against the gate, he reeled back, and fell face upwards to the earth. Our eyes met. He recognised me in a moment. To save his life now was to forfeit my own, and the next moment I plunged the bowie-knife to the hilt in his breast. He gasped out, "This from you, Noah! Poor Elinor, you are terribly avenged!"

He never spoke more. I hastily searched his pockets, and drew from his bleeding breast a large pocket-book, which contained the coveted treasure. I then flung the bloody knife with which I had done the deed to some distance, and fled from the spot, taking a near cut to the lodge across the fields.

I entered at a back gate, and going up to my own room, I carefully washed my bands and face, and dressed myself in the clothes I had worn during the day, thrusting the waggoner's frock and hat, and the fatal pocket-book, into an old sack. I hastily concealed them in a heap of old manure, which had served for a hot-bed in the garden, until a better opportunity occurred of effectually destroying them. All this was accomplished in an almost incredibly short time; and when my arrangements were completed, I once more had recourse to the brandy-bottle, but took good care this time not to take too potent a dose. I then shouldered my gun, and walked to the cottage of the second game-keeper, which lay in my path, and briefly stating my reasons for calling him up, I asked him to accompany me to the second avenue gate to meet my master.

George Norton instantly complied, and we walked together to the appointed spot, discussing in the most animated manner, as we went along, the probable result of the cricket-match at S——.

As we entered the first plantation, we were accosted by Bill Martin and Adam Hows. Both were greatly excited, and exclaimed in a breath,—

"Mr. Carlos has been robbed and murdered! The body is lying just within the second gate, in the middle of the path. Come with us and see!"

"And what brings you here, you scoundrel! at this hour of night?" I cried suddenly, throwing myself upon Bill Martin. "What business have you trespassing in these preserves? If Mr. Carlos is murdered, it is you and your accomplice that have done the deed. It is not pheasants and hares that you came here to shoot, as the muzzle of that pistol, sticking out of your pocket, can prove."

On hearing these words Adam Hows discharged a pistol at my head, and missing his aim, threw down the weapon and fled. Bill Martin struggled desperately in my grasp, but I held him fast. I was a strong, powerful man, and he was enfeebled by constant drunkenness and debauchery. I held him like fate.

Norton now came to my assistance, and we secured Martin's hands with my silk pocket-handkerchief. I remained with my grasp upon his collar, while Norton ran back to the village to fetch the constables.

It was one of the most awful moments in my life, while I stood alone in that gloomy grove confronting my victim. He neither spoke nor trembled. The unhappy man seemed astonished and bewildered at what had befallen him. All was so still around us, that I distinctly heard his heart beat.

We remained in this painful and constrained silence for some time. At last he said in a subdued voice, "Noah Cotton, I am not guilty. I never murdered him."

"Perhaps not. Your comrade in crime may have saved you the trouble."

"Nor him either. The deed was done before we reached the spot."

"What brought you there?" I said, abruptly.

"The hints you threw out for our destruction," and his eye once more flashed with its accustomed boldness. "You acted as decoy-duck, and your superior cunning has triumphed. In order to gratify your old hatred to me, you have killed your benefactor."

The moon was at full but the trees cast too deep a shade upon the spot we occupied to enable him to see my face. I was, however, taken by surprise, and gave a slight start. He felt it, and laughed bitterly.

"We are a pair of d——d scoundrels!" he cried; "but you are the worst, and you know it. I of course must hang for this, for you have laid your plans too well to allow me a loop-hole to escape. Now, Noah Cotton, for once be generous. I know I have treated you confoundedly ill, that I am a very bad fellow, and richly deserve the gallows. But I am very young to die—to die for a crime I did not actually commit. I have a widowed mother, an orphan sister to support, who love me, and will be broken-hearted at my death—for their sakes give me a chance of making my escape. I will leave the country directly, and never return to it again to trouble you more. Have mercy upon me! For Christ's sake have mercy upon me!"

My heart was moved. I was almost tempted to grant his prayer. But I dared not trust him. I knew that my own safety entirely depended upon his destruction.

"William Martin," I said, very calmly, "your attempt to charge me with this crime is a miserable subterfuge. What interest had I to kill Mr. Carlos? Did not my living depend upon him? The folly of the man who killed the goose that laid the golden eggs, would be wisdom compared with such a deed. Mr. Carlos was of more value to me living than dead."

"That is true," he said, thoughtfully. "I may have wronged you. It is a strange inexplicable piece of business." Then he muttered to himself, "'The wages of sin is death.' It is useless to ask mercy from him. He would not save my life if he could. Oh my mother!—my poor, poor mother!"

Hardened as I thought this ruffian had been for years, the big bright drops coursed each other down his sunburnt cheeks; his large chest heaved convulsively, and loud sobs awoke the lone echoes of the wood.

I could endure his agony no longer. "Martin," I said, in a low voice, for the agitation that shook my whole frame nearly deprived me of the power of utterance, "behave more like a man; were you an innocent man, you could not be affected in this strange way."

"By ——, I am not innocent! Who said I was? But I again repeat I did not kill him."

"Then Adam did?"

"No, no—it was his first attempt at murder." He stopped short. He had committed himself.

"Why, Bill, your own words condemn you."

"Don't use them against us. I am mad. I don't know what I say."

"Hush. I hear steps approaching. Be quiet for one moment, while I untie your hands, and I will give you a last chance for your life."

"Your frozen heart has thawed too late," he cried, with a hollow groan. "The constables are already here, and I am a dead man."

He was right; Norton with the constables and a large body of men now burst through the trees. I gladly consigned the prisoner to their charge, while I proceeded with the rest of the party to the spot where the murder had been committed. I knew that it would awaken suspicion for me to remain behind, I therefore placed myself at the head of them; but I would have given worlds to have remained behind. A few minutes brought us to the fatal gate.

We gathered round the body in silence. Horror was depicted on every countenance. Some who had known the 'Squire for years shed tears. I could not; but I gladly buried my face in my handkerchief, to shut out the dreadful spectacle. The moon, peering down between the branches of the trees, looked full in the dead man's face. Those glassy upturned eyes chilled my heart to stone with their fixed icy stare.

Oh! it is terrible to see a man so full of life and health but yesterday, look thus.

"Is he quite dead?" said George Norton. "My poor dear master!—my good generous master! Noah, lend a hand to raise him up."

With a deep groan I seconded his efforts, and the head of the murdered man rested upon my knees. As I crouched beside him on the ground, a viper was gnawing at my heart. I would have given my chance of an eternity of bliss, which not many hours ago I had possessed as man's only true inheritance, to have recalled the transactions of that dreadful night.

"See, here is a wound in his breast," cried I. "He has not been shot, but stabbed with a long sharp dirk or knife. He must have been taken unawares, for he seems to have made no effort to defend himself."

"Here is his hat," cried another. "The back of it is all battered and crushed in. He has been knocked down and then stabbed. Oh, that Martin—that infernal villain!"

Whenever I heard Martin reproached as the murderer, I fancied that those dead eyes of my master looked into my soul with a mournful scorn. Yet I lacked the moral courage to say, "I am the man."

We formed a litter of boughs, and carried the body up to the Hall. We had not proceeded many steps on our sad journey, before Norton stumbled over something in the path. It was the bloody knife.

"Here is something that will give a clue to the mystery. By Jove! Bill Martin's American knife. He was showing this wicked-looking blade and bragging about it the other night at the White Horse. Murder will out. If evidence were wanted of his guilt, this knife would hang him. Faugh! the blood is still wet upon the blade."

The knife passed from hand to hand, and to mine among the rest. I did not see the blood. It appeared to me red-hot—to glow and flicker with the flames of hell.

It was the dawn of day when we reached the Hall with our melancholy burthen. The fatal news had travelled there before us. Half the inhabitants of the village were collected on the lawn. The old servants were standing on the steps to receive the body of their master. As we drew near, cries and groans arose on every side.

"This is a bad job for you, Noah," said the old butler—"for us all; but especially for you. He was your best friend."

"It is a loss to the whole country," I cried, mournfully, shaking my head.

"And Adam Hows is off with the money!" said the steward, with a sharp eager face.

"So we suppose. Martin has been searched, but there is none in his possession. I hope the other rascal will be taken."

"Come with us, Noah, into the kitchen," cried several of the servants in a breath, "and tell us all about it. They say it was you who discovered the murder, and took the villain at the risk of your life. Come in, and take a glass of hot stuff, and give us all the particulars."

And I had to endure a fresh species of torture in recapitulating all the circumstances that I dared reveal of that revolting act; to listen to, and join in all their comments, doubts and surmises, and answer all the agonizing questions suggested by curiosity or compassion. I was beginning to feel hardened to the painful task, and answered their eager inquiries without changing countenance, or betraying more than a decent emotion on the melancholy occasion.

CHAPTER XIX
MY MOTHER

I was relieved from my embarrassing situation by a message from my mother. She was ill, and wished to see me, begging me to return home without a moment's delay.

"Ah, poor woman! This is a sad judgment—a heavy blow to her. She must feel this bad enough," said one of the old servants. "Yes, yes, Noah, lose no time in going home to comfort your mother."

I gazed from one to the other in blank astonishment. They shook their heads significantly. I hurried away without asking or comprehending what they meant.

As I walked rapidly home, I pondered over their strange conduct. Beyond my losing my situation of gamekeeper and porter to the lodge, I could not see in what way the death of Mr. Carlos should so terribly affect my mother, without she suspected that I was his murderer. Guilt is naturally timid; but my plans had been laid with such caution and secrecy, and carried out so well, that it was almost next to an impossibility for her to suspect a thing in itself so monstrously improbable.

The murder had been an impulsive, not a premeditated act. Four-and-twenty hours ago I would have shot the man who could have thought me capable of perpetrating such a deed.

The clocks in the village were striking eight when I entered the lodge. My mother was sitting in her easy chair, supported by pillows. Her face was deathly pale, and she had been crying violently. Two women, our nearest neighbours, were standing by her side, bathing her wrists and temples with hartshorn.

"Oh, Noe," exclaimed Mrs. Jones, "I'm glad thee be come to thy mother. She hath been in fits ever since she heard the dreadful news."

"We could not persuade her that you were safe," said Mrs. Smith. "She will be content when she sees you herself."

"Mother,"—and I went up to her and kissed her rigid brow—"are you better now?"

She took my hand and clasped it tightly between her own, but made no reply. Her face became convulsed, the tears flowed over her cheeks like rain, and she fainted in my arms.

"She is dying!" screamed both women.

"She will be better presently," I said. "Open the window—give me a glass of water! There—there, she is coming to! Speak to me, dear Mother!"

"Is it true, Noah?" she gasped out, but broke down several times before she could make her meaning plain. "Is he—is the Squire dead?—murdered?"

"Too true, Mother! I have just helped to carry the body up to the Hall."

"Oh, oh!" she groaned, rocking herself to and fro in a strange agony; "I hoped it had been false."

"It is a shocking piece of business—but why should it affect you in this terrible way?"

"That's what I say," cried Mrs. Jones. "It do seem so strange to us that she should take on in this here way for a mere stranger."

"Don't ask me any questions, Noah," said my mother, in a low, firm voice. "I am better now. The sight of you has revived me; and these kind neighbours may return home."

"At ten o'clock the magistrates meet at the Market Hall to examine the prisoners," I said, "and I must be there, to make a deposition of what I know. I can stay with you till then."

"Oh, Noe! thee must tell us all about it!" said Mrs. Smith, who was dying with curiosity. "How did it come about?"

I was not prepared for this fresh agony; but I saw that there was no getting rid of our troublesome visitors without endeavouring to satisfy their insatiable greed for news; and I went through the dreadful task with more nerve than I expected. My mother listened to the recital with breathless interest, and the women clung to me with open eyes and mouth, as if their very life depended upon my words, often interrupting me with uncouth exclamations of surprise and horror. At length all was told that I could tell. My mother again broke into passionate tears.

"Poor Mrs. Martin!" she sobbed, "how dreadful it must be to her. I pity her from my very soul!"

I had never given Martin's unfortunate mother a single thought. I was not naturally cruel, and this planted a fresh arrow in my heart.

"It is about eight years ago that she lost her husband," said neighbour Smith. "He died from the bite of a mad dog. He was the 'Squire's gamekeeper then. Little Sally was not born until five months after her father's death. I don't know how the widow has contrived to scratch along, and keep out of the workhouse. But she was always a hard-working woman. She had no friend like the Squire, to take *her* by the hand and give her son a genteel education. She did get along, however, and sent that Bill to Mr. Bullen's school; but she half starved herself to do it—and what good? He has been a world of trouble to her, and almost broke her heart before he run off to 'Meriky. This fresh misfortune will go nigh to kill her outright."

"And was it to add to this poor devoted creature's sorrows," I asked myself, "that I was prepared to give false evidence against her son?" For well I knew, that his life depended upon that evidence.

For Martin I felt no pity. His death never filled me with remorse like the murder of the 'Squire. He was born for the gallows. I had only forestalled him in the deed that would send him to the grave. He had sought the spot with the intention to rob and kill. I had no doubts on that head; and I persuaded myself that he had richly merited the fate that awaited him. But the grief of his unhappy mother awakened a pang in my breast that was not so easily assuaged.

The women at length took their leave, and I was alone with my mother.

For some minutes she remained silent, her hands pressed tightly over her breast, and her tear-swollen eyes fixed mournfully on the ground.

"Noah," she said, at length, slowly raising her head, and looking me earnestly in the face, "do you think that the family would allow me to look at the corpse?"

I actually started with horror. I felt the blood recede from my cheeks, and a cold chill creep from my hair downwards.

"Good God! Mother, what should make you wish to see him? He is a frightful spectacle!—so frightful that I would not look at him again for worlds!"

"Oh," groaned my mother, "it is hard to part from him for ever, without one last look!"

"Mother, Mother!" I cried—while a horrid suspicion darted through, my brain—"what is the meaning of this strange conduct, and still stranger words? In the name of Heaven! what was Squire Carlos to you?"

"Noah, he was your father!" returned my mother, slowly and solemnly. "I need not tell you what he was to me."

Had she stabbed me with a red-hot knife, the effect would have been less painful.

"My father!" I cried, with a yell of agony, as I sank down, stunned with horror, at her feet. "Mother!—Mother! for my sake—for your own sake, recal those dreadful words!"

Some minutes elapsed before I again awoke to the consciousness of my terrible guilt. My crime appeared to me in a new aspect—an aspect that froze my soul, and iced the warm stream of my young blood with despair. I had been excited—agitated—almost maddened, with the certainty of being a murderer; but there was something of human passion in those tumultuous feelings. But the certainty that I was not only a murderer, but a parricide,—had killed my own father for the sake of a few hundred pounds, which I now knew that I could never enjoy, chilled me into a stupid, hardened apathy. There could be no forgiveness for a crime like mine, neither in this world—nor in the world to come.

I could have cursed my wretched mother for having so long concealed from me an important fact, which, if known, had saved the life of her worthless paramour. Her silence might have been the effect of shame. But no—when I recalled the frequency of Mr. Carlos's visits, his uniform kindness to me, the very last conversation I held with him, and the dark hints that from time to time Bill Martin had so insultingly thrown out, I felt convinced that she had all along been living with him on terms of abandoned intimacy, and that her crime had been the parent of my own. Yet, in spite of these bitter recriminations, when I raised my eyes to her, and met her sad, pleading, tearful glance, all my love for her returned, and, clasping her knees, as I still sat upon the ground at her feet, I said, "Mother, why did you keep this guilty secret from me for so many years? I should have felt and acted very differently towards that unhappy man, if I had known that he was my father."

"Noah, it is hard to acknowledge one's sin to one's own child. It is a sin, however, that I have been bitterly punished for committing."

"But you still continued to live on those terms with him?"

"Alas! Noah, I loved him!"

She threw her apron over her head, and sobbed as if her heart would burst.

"I will show you, Mother, how one crime produces another," I was about to say, when a loud rap at the door recalled my self-possession; and I was summoned to attend the sitting of the magistrates, and tell all I knew about the murder.

CHAPTER XX
A LAST LOOK AT OLD FRIENDS

I made my deposition minutely and circumstantially, from the time of my conversation with Adam Hows until the time when, accompanied by George Norton, we encountered him and Bill Martin in the plantations, and took the latter prisoner. My statement was so clear, so plausible, so perfectly matter-of-fact, that this hideous lie was received by wise and well-educated men as God's truth. I heard myself spoken of as a sober, excellent young man, well worthy of the confidence and affection of the 'Squire, and extremely grateful for the many favours he had bestowed upon me; while the character that Martin bore, and his previous pursuits, were enough to condemn him, independently of the startling evidence that I, and others from among his own wild companions, had given against him. A conversation that one of these men had accidentally heard between him and Adam Hows, proclaiming their intention to rob and murder Mr. Carlos, was indeed more conclusive of their guilt than my own account, though that was sufficient to have hung him twice over.

Bill kept his eye fixed on me during the examination. I met it with a degree of outward calmness; but it thrilled me to the soul, and has haunted me ever since. He made no attempt at vindication. He said that the evidence brought against him was circumstantially correct, yet, for all that, neither he nor his accomplice had actually murdered the Squire, and that God, who looked deeper than man, knew that what he said was true.

Of course no one listened to such an absurd statement. But, to cut this painful part of my story short—for it is agony to dwell upon it—he was tried, condemned, and finally executed at ——. I saw him hung.

Yes, Reader, you may well start back from the page in horror. To be sure that my victim was dead, I actually witnessed his last struggles, and returned home satisfied that the tongue I most dreaded upon earth—the only living creature who suspected my guilt—was silenced and cold for ever.

Shallow fool that I was! Conscience never sleeps! The voice of remorse sounds up from the lowest deeps, with the clang of the archangel's trump blasting the guilty ear with its judgment-peal. With him, my peace of mind, self-respect, and hopes of heaven, vanished for ever!

I have since often thought, that God gave me this last chance in order to try me—to see if any good remained in me—if I could for once resist temptation, and act towards Martin as an honest man. I have felt, amid the burning agonies of my sleepless, phantom-haunted nights, that, had I confessed my guilt and saved him from destruction, the same pity that Christ extended to the thief on the cross might have been shown to me.

These dreadful events were the beginning of sorrows. When Mr. Walter came to the Hall to attend his uncle's funeral, and the will of the deceased was opened by the man of business, and read to him after the melancholy ceremony was over, it was found that Mr. Carlos had named me in this document as *his natural son by Anne Cotton,* and had left me the house in which I now live, together with the fifty acres adjoining, and two thousand pounds in the funds. The interest of the latter to be devoted to my mother during her life, but both principal and interest to devolve to me at her death.

This handsome legacy seemed to console my mother a great deal for the loss of her wealthy lover; but it only served to debase me lower in my own eyes, and deepen the pangs of remorse. How gladly would I have quitted this part of the country! but I was so haunted by the fear of detection, that I was afraid lest it might awaken suspicions in the minds of poor neighbours. On every hand I heard that the Squire had made a gentleman of Noah Cotton, while I cursed the money in my heart, and would thankfully have exchanged my lot with the poorest emigrant that ever crossed the seas in search of a new home.

The property bequeathed me by the Squire was a mile from the village, in an opposite direction to the porter's lodge. My mother quitted our old home with reluctance; but I was glad to leave a place which was associated in my mind with such terrible recollections.

The night before we removed to the Porched House—for so my new home was called—I waited until after my mother had retired to her bed, and then carefully removed from its hiding-place the sack and its fatal contents. The waggoner's frock and hat, together with the sack, I burned in a field at the back of the Lodge, and then slunk back, like a guilty wretch, under the cover of night and darkness, to my own chamber. It was some time before I could muster sufficient courage to open the pocket-book. It felt damp and clammy in my grasp.—It had been saturated with his blood; and the roll of bank notes were dyed with the same dull red hue. I did not unroll them. A ghastly sickness stole over me whenever my eye fell upon them. I seemed distinctly to trace his dying face in those horrible stains—that last look of blank surprise and unutterable woe with which he regarded me when he recognised in me his murderer!

It was necessary to put out of sight these memorials of my guilt. I would have burnt them, but I could not bring my heart to destroy such a large sum of money; neither could I dare to make use of it. An old bureau had been purchased by my mother at a sale: she had given it to me, for a receptacle for books and papers. I possessed so few of these, that I generally kept my shooting apparatus in its many odd nooks and drawers. While stowing away these, I had discovered a secret spring, which covered a place of concealment in which some hoarder of by-gone days had treasured a few guineas of the reign of the third George. These I had appropriated to my own use, and had considered them a godsend at the time. Into this drawer I now thrust the bloodstained pocket-book and the useless wealth it contained. Never since that hour have I drawn it from its hiding-place. My earnest wish is, that when I am gone to my last account, this money may be restored to the family to whom it rightfully belongs.

When I settled upon the farm, it afforded me a good pretext to give up my situation as gamekeeper. Mr. Walter, now Sir Walter Carlos, had just come to reside at the Hall, and, being a great sportsman, he was very unwilling to dispense with my services.

"Wait at least, Noah," he said, "until after the shooting-season is over. I expect my sister Ella and her husband and a large party down next week. No one can point out the best haunts of the game like you. This will give me time to procure some one in your place."

I named George Norton as a fitting person to fill the vacant situation. He promised to appoint him in my place, but insisted on my staying with him until the end of October.

Reluctantly I complied. The words he had carelessly spoken respecting his sister, had sent a fresh arrow through my heart. She, for whose sake I had committed that fearful deed, in the hope of acquiring wealth, was now the bride of another. How had I dared to form a hope that one so far removed from me by birth and education would ever condescend to cast one thought on me? Blind fool that I had been! I was conscious of my madness now, when I had forfeited my own soul to obtain the smiles of one who could never be mine.

The gay party arrived in due time at the Hall, and Sir Walter forgot its old possessor, the friend of his boyhood, the gay, roystering, reckless man who slept so quietly in the old churchyard, while pursuing his favourite sport.

Captain Manners, the husband of my beautiful Ella, was a fine, dashing-looking officer, and I felt bitterly jealous of him whenever I saw him and his young bride together. In spite of her sables, she was all smiles and sunshine—the life and soul of the party at the Hall.

One fine afternoon—I shall never forget it!—I was following the gentlemen with the dogs, when we came to the fatal spot where Mr. Carlos had been murdered.

I had never trod that path since the night of his death, though in my dreams I constantly revisited the spot, and enacted the revolting scene in all its terrible details. But there was no avoiding it now. I felt as if every eye was upon me, and I stooped to caress the dogs, in order to conceal the agitation that trembled through my frame.

Just as we drew near the gate, Sir Walter fired at a partridge, which fell among the long fern just at my side.

"Hullo, Noah! pick up that bird. 'Tis a splendid cock," cried Sir Walter.

I parted the fern with trembling hands to do his bidding. The bird lay dead on the very stone over which my unhappy father's life-blood had gushed! I saw the fresh, warm drops that had flowed from the breast of the bird, but, beneath was a darker stain. I tried in vain to lift the creature from the ground. Before me lay the bleeding, prostrate form of Mr. Carlos, with the tender reproach gleaming in his eyes through the deepening mists of death. My senses reeled—I saw no more—I sank down in a fit,—the first of those dreadful epileptic fits which have since been of such constant recurrence.

When I recovered, Sir Walter was supporting me; and Mrs. Manners, who had followed her husband to the field, was fanning me with a small branch of sycamore leaves.

"He's coming to," she said, in a gentle voice. "Why, Noah,"—addressing herself to me—"what ails you?—Were you ever in this way before?"

I answered very faintly, "No; but that I had not been well for some time past. When I stooped to lift the bird, every object seemed to turn round with me, and looked first red and then black: and I remembered nothing more."

"You must be bled, Noah," said Sir Walter, kindly; "this is a clear case of blood to the head. Go home, and I will send Dr. Pinnock to see you as I return to the Hall."

"I am better now," I replied, glancing towards Mrs. Manners, who was regarding me with looks of interest and compassion. "To tell you the truth, Sir Walter, I have not felt like myself since Mr. Carlos was killed. It gave me a dreadful shock. It was on this very spot that he was murdered. That stone is stained with his blood. When I saw it just now, it brought the whole scene so vividly before me, that it made me ill."

"No wonder," said Ella, thoughtfully. "My poor dear uncle! He was the best-hearted man in the world; and was so fond of you, Noah."

"He had a good right to be," returned Sir Walter. "You are not perhaps aware, Ella," he added, in a low voice, "that our friend Noah is his son."

"Indeed!" she cried, in surprise; "that accounts for the affection we both felt for him when a boy,—the interest we feel for him still."

"I wish I was more deserving of your good opinion," I said. "But believe me, Mrs. Manners, I shall retain, during my life, a grateful remembrance of your kindness."

I lifted my hat with profound respect, and looked long and sadly upon her. It was for the last time; for she followed her husband to India, and I never saw her again. Then whistling to my dogs, I pursued my solitary way.

CHAPTER XXI
MY MOTHER AND THE SQUIRE

From that hour I became a prey to constant remorse. My health declined, and my mother at last remarked the change in my appearance; but at that time I am certain she had no idea of the cause.

"Noah," said she, one night, as we were crouching over the fire, for it was winter, and very cold,—"you are much changed of late. You look ill, and out of spirits; you eat little, and speak less. My dear son, what in the world ails you?"

"I am tired of this place, Mother. I should like to sell off, and go to America."

"And leave me for ever?"

"You, of course, would go with me."

"Never!" said my mother, emphatically. "Of all places in the world, I cannot go there."

I looked up inquiringly.

"I will give you my reasons," she continued. "Listen to me, Noah. I have never told you anything about myself; but, before I die, it is only right that you should know all. My husband, whose name you bear, is not, to my knowledge, dead. If living, he is in America."

"Oh, that I had been his son!" I groaned; "but, Mother, proceed—proceed."

"To make matters intelligible to you, it is necessary that I should go back to my early days. I was the only child of a poor shoemaker in St. Alban's. My father was reckoned a good hand at his trade, but he was sadly addicted to drink. For ten years before he died, I never remember his going one night to his bed sober. My poor mother was a neat, quiet little woman, who did all in her power to keep things straight. But first one piece of household furniture went, and then another, until we were left with bare walls and an empty cupboard.

"'Annie,' said my mother, 'this won't do. You must go out and work for your living: you cannot stay at home and starve.'

"'And you, Mother?'

"'God will take care of me, my child. I cannot leave your father. I must work for him: he is my husband; and, in spite of this dreadful vice, I love him still.'

"Her constancy and patient endurance under a thousand privations was wonderful.

"I was reckoned a very pretty girl: all the neighbours said so, and I thought so myself. They were sorry for our altered circumstances. They respected my mother; and, though they blamed my father, they pitied him as well as blamed (he had been a general favourite before he became lost to himself and us,) and did all in their power to assist my mother in her distress. One of these sympathising friends was the dressmaker employed by the great lady of the parish. This woman got me into service as waiting-maid to the young ladies at the Grange.

"Miss Elinor Landsmeer was on the eve of marriage with Mr. Carlos; and she used to talk to me a great deal about her lover, while I was dressing her hair of a night. 'He was so handsome,' she said, 'so good-natured and merry! He danced and sang so well, rode so gallantly, and was such a capital shot. He was admired and courted by all the ladies; and she considered herself the most fortunate girl in the world to have secured the affections of such a charming young man. And then, Annie, besides all these advantages of person and manners, he is so *rich*—so *immensely rich*, he can indulge me in my taste for pictures and books, and dress, without ruining himself. Oh, I shall be so happy—so happy!'—and then she would clap her little white hands, and laugh in childish glee. And very young she was, and very pretty too,—not a showy sort of beauty, but soft and gentle,—not gay and dashing, like some of her elder sisters. They were all engaged to men of rank and fashion; and they laughed at Miss Elinor for marrying an untitled man. But she was so much in love with Mr. Carlos, that she was as happy as a lark.

"When I saw Mr. Carlos, I thought she was, indeed, a fortunate young lady; and I could not help envying her the handsome rich lover who was so soon to make her his wife.

"I always liked waiting on my pretty young lady; but I felt a double pleasure in doing so when Mr. Carlos was by. He often joked Miss Elinor on my good looks, and would ask her 'if she was not jealous of her pretty waiting-maid?'

"'Oh, no,' she would laughingly reply. 'I am like you, Walter,—I don't like ugly people about me. Annie is as good as she looks. Cannot you find a good husband for her among your tenants?'

"'I'll do my best,' said he, in the same bantering tone. 'By the by, Annie—if that is your name—what do you think of my valet, Mr. Noah Cotton?'

"'What an antiquated name!'—and my mistress laughed out. 'Was he brought up in the ark?'

"'Names go by contraries, my dear,' said Mr. Carlos. 'Noah is a deuced handsome fellow; not soft, as his name would imply, but shrewd and clever—as sharp as a needle. I think he would suit Annie exactly; and you and I will stand godfather and godmother for all the little Shems, Hams and Japheths they may happen to place in their ark.'

"'Fie, Walter, fie! You make Annie blush like a rose. Look at him, Annie, the next time he comes in, and tell me what you think of the fine husband Mr. Carlos has provided for you.'

"'Oh, Miss Elinor,' I cried, dropping a low curtsey, 'it is very kind of Mr. Carlos; but I never look at the servants. I am too young to marry.'

"But I did look at Mr. Cotton. He was very attentive to me, and I soon thought him all that his master had said he was. I did not love him, but I foolishly imagined that it was a fine thing to have a sweetheart, and to be married, like my young mistress. And Noah Cotton was a farmer's son, and better educated than most people in our class. He had a good place, and was a great favourite with his master, and could afford to keep me very comfortably. So, when he told me that he preferred me to all the girls he had ever seen, and asked me to marry him, I said that I would consult my mistress, and, if she approved of it, I had not the least objection. Miss Elinor was enchanted with it. She said, it would be capital; that we should be married on the same day with her and Mr. Carlos; that she would buy my wedding-suit, and the Squire would pay the parson the fees; and that we should go with them abroad, in the same capacity we then held.

"And it all took place as she promised. I was dressed in white muslin, trimmed with white ribbons, and just one moss rose-bud in my bosom, and another in my hair. Miss Elinor put them in herself; and then, when I was dressed, she took my hands in hers, and turned me all round, to see that all was neat and nice; and she kissed my forehead, and said that I looked charming,—that any man might be proud of such a little wife; and she called her own bridegroom into her dressing-room, to come and look at me before I went to church.

"Mr. Carlos seemed quite struck with my appearance, and declared 'that I looked as handsome as my mistress; that Noah was a very fortunate fellow; and if he had not been going to marry his own dear Elinor, he would have married me himself.'

"This was all a joke then. My mistress did not like it, however. She did not laugh, and looked very grave for some minutes, and was very hard to please for some days after the wedding.

"It did not strike me then, for I was too happy and too vain to think of anything but myself; but it has often struck me since, that Mrs. Carlos was jealous of me from that hour.

"Mr. Carlos took his bride to Italy, and we went with them to a great many different countries and large cities. It was rather dull for me, for I could not speak the strange outlandish lingo of those foreign lands; and by the time one began to know a few words, we were off to another place, where we were as ignorant as we were before.

"After the first three months of our marriage, my husband grew very cross, and was jealous of every man who spoke civilly to me, though, God knows, at that time I was very fond of him, and never gave him the least cause for his suspicions. He was an obstinate, stern-tempered man, a strict Presbyterian, and very averse to any innocent amusements, in which I greatly delighted. Thus matters went on from day to day, until I not only ceased to love him, but wished, from my very heart, that I had never married him. I no longer tried to please him, but did all in my power to vex and aggravate him, in the hope that he would put a favourite threat of his in practice, and run away and leave me.

"My master always reprimanded my husband when he spoke sharply to me, and told him that he was not worthy of such a treasure; but his interference only made matters worse.

"I often complained to Mrs. Carlos of Noah's cruel treatment, but she always excused him, and said that it was *I* that was to blame; that I made crimes out of every little freak of temper, and that, instead of conciliating my husband, I made the breach wider by insults and reproaches, and took no pains to please him; that if she was to behave in the same way to Mr. Carlos, she should not wonder at his disliking her.

"These observations wounded my pride. I thought them cruel and unjust, and I left her room in tears. Mr. Carlos met me on the stairs. I was crying bitterly, partly out of anger, and partly in the hope of making my mistress sorry for what she had said.

"He asked me what grieved me so, and I told him how I had been treated by Noah, and described in exaggerated terms the reproof I had got from his wife. Mr. Carlos pinched my cheek, and told me to dry my eyes, for crying spoilt my beauty; and not to care for what Noah or my mistress said to me; that he was my friend, and loved and respected me too much to suffer me to be ill-used.

"I felt proud of my master's sympathy, and lost no opportunity to increase it, and attract his attention. You may guess, my son, how all this ended. My master conceived a violent passion for me, which I was not slow in returning, and we carried on our intimacy with such circumspection, that for two years it escaped the vigilant eyes of my husband, and the fretful jealousy of my mistress. The fear of detection made me very cautious in the presence of the injured parties. I appeared more anxious to please my mistress, and more distant and respectful to Mr. Carlos, while I bore with apparent patience and resignation the ill-humour of my now detested husband. For the above-named period, both were deceived, and it was during this season of crime and hypocrisy that you, my son, were born. The startling resemblance you bore to your real father did not escape my husband's observation, and called forth some of his bitterest remarks.

"I, for my part, swore that the child was the image of him; and, in order to lull his suspicions, conferred upon it the odious and hated name of Noah.

"My mistress often visited my chamber during my confinement. Once, she brought Mr. Carlos with her to see the baby. 'It is a beautiful little cherub!' he cried, kissing it, with all his heart in his eyes, 'the picture of Annie.'

"'You will laugh at me, Walter,' said my mistress gravely, 'but I think the child is so like you!'

"She looked at him steadily in the face as she said this. I thought he would have let the babe drop, he did so stammer and colour as he tried to laugh her words off as a good joke. As to me, my face burnt like fire, and I drew up the bed-clothes in order to conceal it. She looked first at me, and then at Mr. Carlos. There needed no further witness of our guilt. We were both convicted by conscience, yet boldly endeavoured to affect indifference.

"'I see how it is,' she said, bursting into tears, 'you have both cruelly wronged me. Yet, for this poor babe's sake, I pray God to forgive you.'

"She kissed the infant with great tenderness (she never had one of her own), laid it in the bed beside me, and withdrew in tears. My heart smote me, and I wept too. The Squire bent over me, and kissing the tears from my eyes, said in a whisper, 'Annie, the cat is out of the bag. My darling, you cannot stay here. I will get a carriage, and take you to London. You will be well taken care of, and I can see you whenever I like, without the painful restraint we are forced to put upon our actions here.'

"I did not answer. I was sorry for my mistress, and ashamed of my own base conduct. At that moment I almost felt as if I hated him.

"It was some days before I was able to be moved from my bed; but I saw my mistress no more. The girl who waited upon me, and who was well paid by Mr. Carlos for her attendance, told me that she was very ill; that the doctor visited her twice a-day, and said that she must be kept very quiet, and nothing said or done to agitate her feelings; that she believed her sickness was occasioned by a quarrel she had had with Mr. Carlos, but she did not know what it was all about; the Squire had left her room in a great rage, and was gone from home for a week.

"I felt certain that I was the cause of this illness, and that the quarrel was about me, which made me very anxious to leave the house.

"That evening my husband came in to see me. He had been drinking freely. He sat down by the bed-side, and looked cross and moodily at me. The baby began to cry, and I asked him to hold it for me for a minute.

"'The hateful brat!' he said, 'I would rather wring its neck.'

"'What an affectionate father!' I cried.

"'Father!' he burst out in a voice of thunder. 'Will you dare to call *me* the father of this child?'

"'Of course it is your child.'

"'Annie, 'tis a base lie,' he said, bending down to my pillow, and hissing the words into my ear. 'Mr. Carlos is the father of this child, and you cannot look me in the face and deny it. Has not God brought against you a witness of your guilt in the face of this bastard, whom you have called by my name, to add insult to injury? I could kill both you and it, did I not know that that would be but a poor revenge. No; live to deserve his scorn as you have done to deserve mine, and may this child be your punishment and curse!'

"I cowered before his just and furious anger. I saw it was useless longer to deny the truth, still more useless to entreat his forgiveness for the injury I had done him; and I drew a freer breath when he tauntingly informed me, 'that this meeting was our last. That he no longer looked upon me as his wife; that he had loved me faithfully, and I had dishonoured him; and he had taken his passage for America, and would leave England for ever the next morning.'

"He was true to his word. He left me, with hatred in his heart and scorn upon his lips, and I have never heard from him or seen him since.

"Mr. Carlos and I rejoiced at his departure, for he was the only person from whose anger we had anything to dread. My poor mistress suffered in silence. She never made her wrongs known to her own family or to the world.

"Mr. Carlos hired lodgings for me in London, where I lived until his wife died, which event took place a few weeks after I quitted the house. Her death, for awhile, greatly affected the Squire, and for several months he appeared restless and unhappy. Once he said to me very sorrowfully,—it was a few days after her funeral,—'Annie, my wife was an angel. My love for you broke her heart. With her last breath she forgave me, and begged me to be kind to you and the child. I was not worthy of her. I wish from my very soul that I had never seen you.'

"These words made me very unhappy, for I adored Mr. Carlos, and dreaded the least diminution of his regard; and I could not help feeling deep remorse for the share I had had in the untimely death of my beautiful young mistress. I grew sad and melancholy, and Mr. Carlos, who really loved me and my child better than anything in the world, and would have married me had my husband's death rendered that event possible, brought me down to F——, and established me at the porter's lodge, where he could see and converse with me every day. It was well known in the neighbourhood on what footing I stood with the Squire, though you, my poor boy, never suspected the fact. You may now perceive, Noah, how great has been our loss in Mr. Carlos. I have lost a kind friend and protector, a husband in everything but the name, and you an affectionate friend and father. Do not urge me to leave this place. When I die I wish my bones to lie in the same churchyard with his, although his rank hinders me from sharing his grave."

My mother ceased speaking, and sat with her hands folded complacently in her lap, and I glared upon her for some time in gloomy silence. She appeared tranquil, scarcely conscious of the crimes she had committed. Was she not as much a murderess as I was a murderer, with only this difference, that I had struck my victim suddenly and quickly,—she had tortured hers for two whole years, until she sank broken-hearted into her grave; and had not her sin been the parent of my own? Then I thought of her husband's terrible curse, "May that child live to be your punishment!" Was not the fearful prediction already fulfilled, although she was ignorant of it? I cannot say that I felt glad that she was no better than her son, but it seemed a palliation of my own guilt.

My mother was annoyed by my long silence. "What are you thinking about, Noah?"

"The shocking story you have just told me. I did not think it possible, Mother, that you could be so bad."

"What do you mean?" she cried out angrily.

"I mean what I say. If this story does not lower you in your own eyes, it does in mine. Mother, I have always respected and venerated you till this moment; I can do so no longer. For, mark me, Mother, as the tree is, so is the fruit. How can you expect me, the offspring of such guilt, ever to be a good man?"

"Noah, this is strange language from you! Thank God! you have done nothing at present to cause me shame or reproach."

"You don't know what I have done—what this confession of yours may tempt me to do. God knows, I would rather have been the son of the despised and injured man whose name I bear, than the bastard of the silken reprobate it was your shame to love."

"Oh, Noah! do not speak thus of your own father."

"Curse him! He has already met with his reward. And your sin, Mother, will yet find you out."

I sprang from my chair to leave the room: my mother laid her hand upon my arm: her eyes were brimful of tears.

"Noah, I have not deserved this treatment from you. Whatever my faults may have been, I have been a kind mother to you."

She looked so piteous through her tears that, savage as I felt, my heart reproached me for my harsh, cruel speech. I kissed her pale cheek and sighed, "I forgive you, my poor mother. I would that God could as easily pardon us both; but He is just as well as merciful, and we are great sinners."

She looked enquiringly at me, as I lighted the candle, and strode up to bed.

CHAPTER XXII
EVIL THOUGHTS—THE PANGS OF REMORSE

All day I toiled hard on my farm to drown evil thoughts. If I relaxed the least from my labour, the tempter was ever at hand, urging me to commit fresh crimes; and night brought with it horrors that I dared not think of in the broad light of day. I no longer cared for wealth. The hope of distinguishing myself in the world had died out of my heart. But industry always brings a reward for toil, and in spite of my indifference, money accumulated, and I grew rich.

My household expenses were so moderate, (for I shunned all society,) that every year I put by a large sum, little caring hereafter by whom it might be spent. My mother sometimes urged me to marry; but I slighted her advice on that head. The history of her wedded life was enough to make me eschew the yoke of matrimony.

My old craze for leaving the country was still as strong as ever; but I had given a solemn promise to my mother to remain in England as long as she lived. Often as I sat opposite to her in the winter evenings, I wished it would please God to take her. It was very wicked; but I never could meet her eyes without fearing lest she should read my dreadful secret in the guilty gloom of mine. I had loved her so devotedly when a boy, that these sinful thoughts were little less than murder.

There was one other person whom I always dreaded to meet, and that was Mrs. Martin, the mother of my unfortunate victim. This woman never passed me on the road without looking me resolutely in the face. There was a something which I could scarcely define in her earnest regard; it was a mixture of contempt and defiance, of malignity, and a burning thirst for revenge. At any rate, I feared and hated her, and wished her either dead or out of my path.

Fortunately for me, she heard of a situation likely to suit her in a distant parish, but lacked the means to transport herself and her little daughter thither. I was so eager to get rid of her, that I sent her anonymously ten pounds to further that object. My mother and her gossips imagined the donation came from the Hall, and were loud in their praises of Sir Walter, and his generous present to the poor widow. But Sir Walter Carlos had no such motives as mine to stimulate his bounty.

It was just about this period that I fell sick of a dangerous and highly infectious fever. The house was of course deserted. The doctor and my mother were the only persons who approached my sick-bed; the latter had all the fatigue and anxiety of nursing me herself, and she did not shrink from the task.

The good, the happy, the fortunate, the lovely, and the beloved, those to whom life is very dear, and the world a paradise, die, and are consigned by their weeping friends and kindred to the dust. But a despairing, heaven-abandoned, miserable wretch like me, struggled through the horrors of that waking night-mare of agony, the typhus fever, and once more recovered to the consciousness of unutterable woe.

Delirium, like wine, lays bare the heart, and shows all its weakness and its guilt, revealing secrets which the possessor has for half a life carefully hid. This, I doubt not, was my case, although no human lip ever revealed to me the fact.

When I left my bed, I found my mother gliding about the house, the very spectre of her former self. Her beautiful auburn hair, of which she was so proud, and which, when a boy, I used to admire so much in its glossy bands, was as white as snow. Her bright blue loving eye had lost all its fire, and looked dim and hopeless, like the eyes of the dead. Alarmed at her appearance, I demanded if she was ill.

She shook her head, and said, "that her anxiety during my illness had sadly pulled her down. But I need not ask any questions. God had humbled her greatly. Her sin had found her out." And then she hurried from me, and I heard her weeping hysterically in her own room.

"Could I have betrayed myself during the ravings of fever?" I trembled at the thought; but I dared not ask.

From that hour no confidence existed between me and my mother. During the day I laboured in the field, and we saw little of each other. At night, we sat for hours in silence—I with a book, and she with her work—without uttering a word. Both seemed unwilling to part company and go to bed, but we lacked the moral courage to disclose the sorrow that was secretly consuming us.

Years passed on in this cheerless manner—this living death. My mother at length roused herself from the stupor of despair. She read the Bible earnestly, constantly; she wept and prayed, she went regularly to chapel, and got what the Methodists call religion. Her repentance was deep and sincere; she gradually grew more cheerful, and would talk to me of the change she had experienced, urging me, in the most pathetic manner, to confess my sins to God, and sue for pardon and peace through the blood of the Saviour. My heart was closed to conviction. I could neither read nor pray. The only thing from which I derived the least comfort was in sending from time to time large sums of money anonymously to Sir Walter Carlos, to relieve him from difficulties to which he was often exposed by his reckless extravagance.

The beautiful Ella, the idol of my boyhood and youth, died in India. I heard the news with indifference; but when I saw the lovely orphan girl she had left to the guardianship of her brother, I wept bitter tears, for she reminded me of her mother at the same sinless age; and the sight of her filled my mind with unutterable anguish, recalling those days of innocent glee that the corrosive poison of guilt had blotted from my memory.

My paradise was in the past, but the avenging angel guarded the closed gates with his flaming sword. My present was the gulf of black despair; my future was a blank, or worse. Oh, agony of agonies!—how have I contrived to endure so much, and yet live?

Death! The good alone can contemplate death with composure. Guilt is a dreadful coward. The bad dare not die. My worst sufferings are comprised in this terrible dread of death. I have prayed for annihilation; but this ever-haunting fear of after punishment forbids me to hope for that. The black darkness—the soul-scorching fire—the worm that never dies—the yells of the damned—these I might learn to endure; but this hell of conscience—this being cast out for ever from God and good—what obstinacy of will could ever teach me to bear this overwhelming, increasing sense of ill?

Ten long years have passed away; the name of Squire Carlos is almost forgotten. People used to talk over his death at alehouses, and by the roadside, but they seldom speak of him now. A splendid monument covers his mouldering dust. The farmers lounge around it on the Sabbath, and discuss their crops and the news of the village. They never glance at the marble slab, or read the tale it tells. The old Hall has passed into other hands. Sir Walter dissipated his inheritance, and died childless in a distant land. The lovely little girl is gone, no one knows whither. The homage of the rising generation is paid to the present Lord of the Manor, and the glory of the once proud family of Carlos is buried in the dust with the things that were.

Why cannot I, too, forget? This night—the anniversary of the accursed night on which I first shed blood, and that the blood of a father, is as vividly impressed upon my mind as though ten long years had not intervened!

How terribly long have they been to me! Is there no forgiveness for my crime? Will God take vengeance for ever?

My mother still lives, but her form droops earthward. Sad, silent, and pale, her patient endurance is my perpetual reproach. I feel that my crime is known to her, that her punishment is as terrible as my own. I took up her Bible the other day from the little table on which she had left it, and unclosing the volume, my eyes were arrested by these awful words,—"The seed of the adulterous bed shall perish." I felt that I was doomed—that the sins of my parents had been visited on me; and the horrible thought brought consolation. I am but a passive instrument in the hands of an inexorable destiny. Why continue this struggle with fate? Conscience will not be cheated. Night came, and the delusion vanished: the horrors of remorse are upon me. I feel that I am responsible for the acts done in the flesh, "that as a man sows, so must he reap." The burden of my soul is intolerable; when shall I find rest?

Another year has vanished into the grave of time. My mother, my poor mother, is at last gone. She died calmly and full of hope. She told me that she knew all—had known it since my illness. The sad conviction of my guilt at first plunged her in despair, then brought repentance, and repentance hope, forgiveness, peace. She had wept and prayed for me for years. She trusted that I should yet find mercy through my Saviour's blood.

It was not until she lay dead before me, that I knew how dear she was,—what a dreadful blank her absence made in my home. I no longer had her eye to dread; but, like the little children who huddle together in the dark, was afraid of being alone,—afraid, even in noon-day, of something I knew not what.

Benjamin, the old servant who has lived with me ever since I came to the Porched House, grieves with me over the loss of a kind mistress. I used to be sullen and reserved to honest Ben; I am glad to talk to him for companionship. My dog, too, has become inexpressibly dear; he sleeps at the foot of my bed at night. Oh, that he could scare away the demons that haunt my pillow! Ben advises me to take a wife. He says that I should be happier with a young woman to look after the house. He may be right. But, alas! what can I do? Will any woman whom I could love, condescend to unite her destiny with an old care-worn man like me? The iron hand of remorse has bent my once active figure, and turned my dark locks grey before my time. How can I ask a young girl to love and obey me?

Tush!—I have wealth,—who knows my guilt? Have I not kept the secret for years? Can I not keep it still? A good woman might lead me to repent, and teach me how to pray.—I will marry.

Providence, if Providence still watches over a wretch like me, has thrown a lovely, simple girl in my way. The evil spirit was upon me, the wrath of God spoke in tones of thunder, and the murdered stood visibly before me face to face. Nature and reason yielded to the shock, and the fatal secret trembled on my lips. In that hour of mental agony, she did not disdain to take me to her humble home, to soothe and comfort the fear-stricken stranger. My heart is melted with love and gratitude. I feel a boy once more, and the sins of my manhood are lost in the dim shadows of bygone years.

She is mine! She regards me as her benefactor. My Sophy, my darling wife! she is the good angel sent by a relenting God to snatch me from perdition! My heart cleaves to my new-found treasure; and, wonder of wonders! she loves me. Loves me—the murderer! While her arms encircle me, the hot breath of the fiend ceases to scorch my brain.

My felicity has been of short duration. The mother of Martin has returned, and is living in our immediate neighbourhood. This bodes me no good. The raven of remorse is again flapping her black wings around my head. My sleep is haunted by frightful dreams. "There is no peace for the wicked." The sight of this woman fills me with dismay.

My wife is unhappy. She does not complain, but her cheeks are deadly pale, and she is wasted to a shadow. I dare not inquire the cause of her grief. I remember the sad, patient face of my mother, and I tremble lest Sophy has discovered my guilt.

Oh God! she knows it all. She asked me a question yesterday that has sealed my doom. Instead of falling at her feet, and pouring out the sorrows of my heart, I spoke harshly to her—even threatened to strike her if she alluded to the subject again. Will she be able to keep the dreadful secret? I tremble before a young girl,—I dare not meet her eyes. If she breathes a word to the mother of Martin, I am lost.

Here the felon's manuscript abruptly terminated. Sophy still held it tightly in her hand, although her eyes, now blinded with tears, were unable to trace a single letter of the concluding page.

"My poor husband!" at last she sobbed, "the punishment of Cain was light when compared with yours. Oh! let me hope that He, who willeth not the death of a sinner, has accepted your repentance and pardoned your sin."

A gentle grasp was laid upon the shoulder of the mourner; and she looked up into the dark expressive face of her deformed sister.

She too had her tale of sorrow. Their mother was dead, but her end was peaceful and full of humble hope, and Mary, the pious Mary, could not wish her back. She had no home now,—she had come to share the home of her more fortunate sister. At first, she could not comprehend the cause of Sophy's tears, of her deep distress; for the news of Noah Cotton's arrest and death had not reached her, while in close attendance upon the obscure death-bed of her mother.

What a mournful history Sophy had to tell; and how deeply Mary sympathised in all her afflictions! Left in comfortable and even affluent circumstances, (for the lawyer employed to wind up Noah Cotton's affairs found that he had large sums invested in several banks, and all his property was willed to his wife,) Sophy was no longer haunted by the dread of poverty, but she often was heard to say with a sigh, that poverty, though a great evil, was not the greatest she had had to contend with; that much as she had in former days murmured over her humble lot while working for daily bread, she was far happier than in the possession of wealth, that had been acquired by dishonest means, and which might emphatically be called *The wages of sin!* "A little that the righteous hath, is better than great riches of the ungodly."

CHAPTER XXIII
TRUST IN GOD

A few words more, and my tale is ended.

The death of Noah Cotton, fraught as it was with agony to his wife, was the means of rescuing the child of his first love, Ella Carlos, from ruin—the little girl, whose striking likeness to her mother had made such an impression on the mind of her unfortunate and guilty lover. After the death of Sir Walter Carlos, who was the last of his name, and, saving the young Ella Manners, his sister's orphan child, the last of his race, the estate at F—— was sold to pay his debts, and the noble property, that had been for several ages in the family, passed into the hands of strangers. The young Ella, left dependent upon the charity of an aunt of her fathers, married the curate of a small parish not many miles from H——, in the county of S——. The match was one of pure affection; the beautiful young girl brought no fortune to her husband. Mr. Grant's income was less than 150*l.* per annum; but in the eyes of love, it seemed sufficient for all their wants. Several years passed away, and the young couple, though obliged to dispense with most of the luxuries of life, did not repent the imprudent step they had taken.

Ella was the happy mother of three fine children, and she nearly doubled her husband's slender income by teaching a small but select school. At length the day of trial came. Mr. Grant was taken ill, and was obliged to relinquish his parochial duties. Ella's time was devoted entirely to her sick husband. The school was broken up, and after a long and severe affliction, which consumed all their little savings, the curate died deeply regretted by his flock, by whom he was justly beloved; and such was the poverty of his circumstances, that his funeral, and decent mourning for his wife and children, were furnished by subscription. After the melancholy rite was over, the widow found herself and her young children utterly destitute.

"I have hands to work—I must not despair," said she, as she divided the last morsel of bread she had among the children, reserving none for herself; "I have trusted in God all my life, and though it has come to this, I will trust in His mercy yet."

She sat down by the window, and looked sadly towards the churchyard. She could scarcely, as yet, realize the truth, that her husband was sleeping there, and that she, the cherished idol of his heart, had prayed for daily bread from the great Father, and was fasting from sheer want. It was a bleak cold day,—the autumnal wind was stripping the sallow leaves from the trees, and roaring like a hungry demon among the shivering branches; a little sparrow hopped upon the window-sill, and relieved his hunger by picking up some grass seeds that the children had gathered in the ear; and left by accident there,—and while the poor mourner watched the bird through her tears, the text so touchingly illustrating the providential care of the Creator, recurred to her memory—"Fear not, ye are of more value than many sparrows,"—and she dried the tears from her eyes, and felt comforted.

The postman's sharp rap at the door roused her from her vision of hope and trust, and she was presented with a letter. Alas! the postage was unpaid, to her, who had not a single penny. This was a severe disappointment.

"John Hays, I cannot take in the letter."

"Why not, Ma'am, I'm sure 'tis directed to you."

"Yes, but I have no money: I cannot pay the post."

"'Tis only a shilling."

"It might as well be a pound, John. You must take it back."

"No, Ma'am, that's just what John Hays won't do. I arn't over rich myself, but I will trust you with the shilling, and take my chance. That letter may bring you news of a forten."

Mrs. Grant read the letter; honest John, leaning against the open door, eyed her all the while. At length she clasped her hands together, and burst into tears.

"Oh lauk! oh lauk!" he cried, shaking his head; "there's no luck arter all."

Mrs. Grant shook him heartily by the hand. "Your money is safe, John; the letter does contain good news—news most unexpected and surprising. Thanks be to God! no one ever trusted Him in vain."

The letter which gave such relief to her mind was from the lawyer employed by Mrs. Cotton in arranging her husband's affairs. It apprised Mrs. Grant of the sum of money found after his death in Noah Cotton's bureau, to which she was the lawful heir, and requesting her for the necessary documents, that would enable him to transfer it to her.

This unhoped-for piece of good fortune enabled Mrs. Grant to emigrate with her children to Lower Canada, where a brother of Mr. Grant's had been settled for some years. She opened a school in one of the principal towns, and became a rich and prosperous woman.

Her eldest son is now a surgeon in good practice; her youngest a pious minister; her daughter the wife of a respectable merchant. In the hour of adversity, let us cling close to the Great Father, and he will not leave us without daily bread.

CHAPTER XXIV
FISHING ON THE BANKS

Flora finished her story, but she wanted courage to read it to her husband, who was very fastidious about his wife's literary performances. And many long years passed away, and they had known great sorrows and trials in the Canadian wilderness, before she again brought the time-worn manuscript to light, and submitted it to his critical eye.

And because it pleased him, she, with the vanity natural to the sex, to say nothing of the vanity so common to the author, thought that it might find favour with the public.

They had just reached the banks of Newfoundland, when she commenced writing Noah Cotton, and the ship still lay there in rain and fog, when she brought it to a close.

The condition of the *Anne* and her passengers was little to be envied. In the steerage, the provisions of the emigrants were nearly exhausted, and the allowance of execrable water was diminished to a pint a day per head. Famine already began to stare them in the face. They had been six weeks at sea, and the poorer emigrants had only provided necessaries for that period. The Captain was obliged to examine the stores which still remained, and to charge the people to make the most sparing use of them until they made land.

The improvident, by this time, were utterly destitute, and were fed by the Captain, who made them pay what little they could towards their support. This, Mr. Lootie told them, was an act of tyranny, for the Captain was bound to feed them, as long as he had a biscuit in the ship. Indeed, he lost no opportunity of fostering dissentions between Boreas and his people; and the difficult position in which the old sailor was placed was rendered doubly so, by the mischievous and false representations of this base-minded man.

The poor emigrants grew discontented, as their wants daily increased, and had no longer spirits to dance and enjoy themselves; yet some sort of excitement seemed absolutely necessary, to keep their minds from preying upon themselves and each other.

Now would have been the time for Mr. S— —to have proved his Christian ministry, and tried by his advice, and the gentle application of that unerring balsam for all diseases of mind and body, the Word of God, to reconcile these poor people to their situation, and teach them to bear with fortitude the further trials to which they might be exposed. But at this critical period of the voyage, he kept aloof, and seldom made his appearance upon the deck, or if he did steal out for a constitutional promenade, he rarely exchanged a salutation with the passengers.

Not so Mr. Lootie. The little brown man had roused himself from his lair, and was all alive. He might constantly be seen near the forecastle, surrounded by a set of half-famished young fellows, enjoying a low species of gambling, well known to school-boys as "Pitch and Toss," "*Chuck Farthing*," and other equally elegant terms, quite worthy of the amusement.

There are some minds so base, that they only require a combination of circumstances, to show to what depths of meanness they can stoop. Mr. Lootie's was a mind of this class. He felt no remorse in replenishing his pockets from the scanty resources of these poor emigrants, joining in the lowest species of gambling in order to win their money, part of which, as a sort of excuse to himself, he expended in liquor, in order to reconcile his victims to their loss; for, with very few exceptions, he was always the winner.

Even the solitary sixpence, the sole fortune of the brothers Muckleroy, found its way into the pocket of the rapacious defaulter.

Flora watched these proceedings until she could control her indignation no longer, and accosting Mr. Lootie on deck, she remonstrated with him on his immoral and most ungentlemanly conduct. He replied, with a sneer, "They were fools. He had as much right to take advantage of their folly as another. Some one would win their money if he did not. The people were hungry and disappointed; they wanted amusement, and so did he; and he was not responsible to Mrs. Lyndsay, or any one else, for his conduct."

Flora appealed to his conscience.

The man had no conscience. It had been hardened and rendered callous long years ago, in the furnace of the world; and she turned from his coarse unfeeling face with sentiments of aversion and disgust.

She next tried to warn his simple victims against venturing their little all in an unequal contest with an artful, designing man. In both cases her good intentions were frustrated. The want of employment, and the tedium of a long, dull voyage, protracted under very unfavourable circumstances, an insufficiency of food and water, the want of the latter in particular rendering them feverish and restless, made the emigrants eager for any diversion sufficiently exciting to rouse them from the listless apathy into which many of them were fast sinking. They preferred gambling, and losing their money, to the dulness of remaining inactive; and the avarice of their opponent was too great to yield to a woman's arguments. Mr. Lootie was a person who held dogs and women in contempt, and in return, he was hated and defied by the one, and shunned and disliked by the other; the unerring instinct of the dog, and the refined sensibility of the woman, keenly discriminating the brutal character of the man.

In the cabin, the Lyndsays fared very little better than the emigrants in the steerage. Tea, sugar, and coffee were luxuries no longer to be thought of; they just lasted the six weeks; and one morning Sam Fraser, with a rueful face, displayed the empty tea-pot, and conveyed the melancholy intelligence that "they were out of everything fit for Christians to eat or drink."

"Can't be helped, Sam," said the Captain, shrugging his shoulders. "We may be thankful that things arn't worse. There is still water in the hold."

"Not much of that either, Sir. It's just the colour of tea, Sir—if it had but the flavour."

"*If*"—ah! that terrible if. What a difference it made to all concerned in its introduction into that sentence—"*if* it had but the flavour!" The smell of the water, when it entered the cabin, was bad enough to sicken the keenest appetite; it was sufficiently disgusting to make the strongest individual there wish that he had no nose, no taste, no recollection of a better and purer element, while drinking it. The water was dead, corrupt, and had been so for the last fortnight; but it was all they had wherewith to slake their thirst.

The breakfast this morning was reduced to a small plateful each of oatmeal porridge, made with the said *rich* water, with porter or Edinburgh ale for sauce.

A very little of this strong food satisfied Flora. The Captain and Lyndsay pronounced it "not bad;" while poor James Hawke ate it, with the tears running down his cheeks into his plate, to the great amusement of Boreas, who told him "that he had discovered a sauce for stirabout he never saw eaten before."

They had scarcely concluded their scanty meal, when Sam presented the Captain with a dirty, three-cornered note, which, he said, Mr. Lootie had ordered him to deliver *instantly*!

"What's in the wind now?" said the old sailor. "I'm not a very good scribe, and the fellow writes such a cramped fist that I can't make it out. Do, Mrs. Lyndsay, oblige me by reading it."

The note was very brief, very insolent, and certainly to the point. The S, which commenced the Sir that headed the missive, had a most forbidding appearance. The loop was formed like the lash of a horsewhip, and reached half down the epistle; thus—

> "Sir,—I demand the use of the tea-pot! as part of our agreement. If this is longer denied, I shall look upon you as an infernal, swindling, old scoundrel!!!
>
> "James Lootie.
>
> "August 16, 1832.
>
> Brig *Anne*.

"He may be d—d!" cried Boreas, in an ecstasy of rage. "But that's too good for him. Many an honest fellow meets with that fate, who would scorn to speak to such a low, mean, pitiful thief!"

"Don't put yourself into such a passion, Captain," said Lyndsay. "The man does not deserve it; it would gratify him to know that he could annoy you by his impertinence. Just send Sam up with the empty tea-pot, and your compliments, and tell him that the tea is all out, and he is quite welcome to the use of the pot for the rest of the voyage."

"Ha, ha!" said the Captain, rubbing his hands; "that's the way to exasperate him. Thank you, Mr. Lyndsay, for the suggestion. Go, Sam, and make the experiment."

In a few minutes Sam returned with a very rueful face, holding his hand to his head, minus the tea-pot.

"Well, what did the rascal say?"

"He broke my head with the tea-pot; and worse than that, Sir, it will be of no further use to any one, for he pitched it into the sea, and wished us both in h——."

"Very civil, truly. And what did you say?"

"Thanked him for his good wishes, and hoped that we might have a pleasant voyage. You know, Sir, I am deaf of one ear, and I pretended to misunderstand him, on purpose to anger him the more. But he let out, and swore loud enough to make the dead hear."

"Were you born deaf, Sam? or did you owe it to sickness or accident?" said Flora.

"Why, Ma'am, that's rather a hard point to determine. It was a queer way in which I lost my hearing," said honest Sam, with a grin; "I'm sure it will make you laugh when I tell you how it happened, but it is true for all that. My old grandmother, who brought me up (for my father and mother died when I was very young), was a pious woman, and very anxious that I should turn out a good boy. She made me attend the Sunday-school regularly, and beat me soundly if I dared to stay away unknown to her. We used to learn texts from the Scriptures, which were printed on small thin pieces of pasteboard. One day, instead of learning my text, which was very hard, and the weather was hot, and I felt particularly lazy, I put it into my ear, and pretended that I had lost it, when the teacher called me up to say my task. I don't know how I contrived it, but I had thrust it in so far that I could not get it out; and I was afraid to tell Granny what had happened. This brought on an inflammation in my ear, which nearly cost me my life. The doctor extracted the text, but I have been deaf o' that ear ever since."

"And the text?" demanded James Hawke; "was it—'Those who have ears to ear, let them hear?'"

"I should rather think," said Flora, "it must have been—'Like the deaf adder that stoppeth her ears, and refuseth to hear the voice of the charmer, let him charm never so wisely.'"

"I don't remember what it was," replied Sam; "but I have been severely punished for my idleness and folly."

"I think that you are all suffering for my folly just now," said Boreas, "when I consented to take that insolent reptile, Lootie, on board. I have no doubt that all our misfortunes are owing to him."

"Don't dignify him into a second Jonah, Captain."

"Ah, how I should like to pitch the little wretch overboard! But hang me if there's a shark or a whale in the great deep that would condescend to swallow such a tough, ill-favoured, cross-grained, pitiful rascal!"

Shortly after this colloquy in the cabin, the parties went on deck. Mr. Lootie was, as usual, diverting himself with the steerage passengers. As the Captain passed the group of gamblers, the men left off their amusement, and scowled upon him, as if they considered him in the light of a common enemy; while Lootie, quitting the game, strutted up to him with an air of insolent defiance.

"What's the meaning of your conduct to me, Captain Williams, this morning? Are you going to starve me, as you are starving the rest of the people? Why was not my tea sent to me as usual?"

"Simply because there is none; and you must go without, like your neighbours," said Boreas, making a strong effort to control his passion before the people.

"You are a liar and a cheat!" yelled the little brown man. "I have paid for these things, and I will have them!"

"Shut up directly," said Boreas, walking straight up to him, "or I will have you put in irons as a runaway thief, and deliver you over to the proper authorities the moment we reach Quebec. You may thank your stars that you are here, and not in gaol."

The little man snarled, and drew back, without daring to make a reply. The emigrants exchanged glances. Some laughed, others shrugged their shoulders, while Stephen Corrie said, aloud—

"I told you, boys, while he was making mischief between you and the Captain, that he was nobody. Now I hope you'll believe me."

"He's a mean chap," muttered another; "he has cheated me out of all my money."

"And me," "and me," chimed in several voices. "If the Captain gave him his deserts, he would pitch him overboard."

"That's what we'll do, my hearties, and send him to look after my tea-pot, if he gives us any more of his jaw," cried Boreas, as Lootie slunk away to take refuge in his boat. "When you listen to such a fellow as that, you should be sure that he is your friend. He tries to make bad blood between us, to serve his own ends, and rob you of your little property. Now, mark me, lads; I'll have no more of this gambling carried on in the ship, and I'll make a public example of the first man that dares to disobey my orders."

"Hurrah, Captain!" cried Stephen. "It's a pity you did not come to that determination a fortnight ago; it would have saved several here from ruin."

"Hold your tongue, Stephen Corrie. It's not for you to brag," cried the Glasgow lad. "You may well be more virtuous than the rest of us, when you have nothing to lose."

"True for you, my boy!" returned Stephen, laughing, "I only follow the way of the world; and preach morality when I'm beyond the reach of temptation."

The next day happened to be Sunday. The calm continued; but the fog was not quite so dense, and the sun made several efforts to show his face, and dispel the haze. Flora was leaning over the side of the vessel, looking intently at some sea-weed floating upon the glassy surface of the sea, when a large grampus flung himself quite out of the water, cut a most absurd caper in the air, and having accomplished a summerset, evidently to his own satisfaction, plunged once more head foremost into the deep.

"Ay, Mistress Lyndsay! what an awful length o' a beast!" said a shrill voice at Flora's elbow, and she looked down into the shrivelled-up face of old Granny Williamson.

"Did ye ever see the like o' that?"

"It was very amusing," said Flora.

"Hout, woman, it makes a' my flesh creep; sure the deevil has the fashioning o' they fearsome things."

Before the old woman could communicate any more original remarks, the Captain came up, and told Mrs. Lyndsay that it was a capital day for fishing; and though it was the Sabbath, he thought that, as they were situated, they should not lose an opportunity of trying to increase their scanty stock of provisions.

Flora perfectly agreed with old Boreas, and he went among the people to see if any of them were provided with tackle. Only two fishing-hooks and lines could be discovered among the whole ship's crew. One of these was the property of Mr. Wright, the second mate, and the two Muckleroys held a joint partnership in the other.

The Captain baited the hooks with a piece of pork, and set Sobersides to fish on one side of the vessel, while he tried his luck on the other, Flora standing by him, feeling the greatest interest in the success of the parties, who had made an agreement to divide equally among the passengers the fish it might be their good fortune to capture.

It has often been said "that a watched pot takes long to boil;" and for a very long time, the many eyes that looked down with eager expectancy on the water, looked and watched in vain.

"Confound the fish!" cried old Boreas, losing patience, "why don't they bite."

"They might give you two reasons, Captain," said Corrie, who was standing by; "Either they are not hungry, or have no appetite for salt pork."

"In the latter case, I should consider them fish of taste," said Lyndsay.

"I could give you a better reason," said a hoarse voice near. All started, and turned their eyes upon the speaker: it was the preacher. "It is because you are desecrating the Sabbath, and breaking the commandments of God. How can you expect a blessing to follow such impious conduct, Captain Williams? I am astonished at a man of your age setting such a terrible example to your passengers and crew."

"Hold your gab!" cried Boreas, "and stand out of the way. He who feeds the ravens when they call upon Him, has sent the hungry a blessing in the shape of a large fish. My eyes! what a whopper! Hurrah, my lads!—here's something to eat!"

The great cod leaped and floundered upon the deck; flapping the women's feet with its slimy tail, and coming rather unceremoniously in contact with the religious professor's black pants.

"A fish! a fish! The Captain has caught a big fish!" cried all the children in chorus. The women clapped their hands—the hungry men laughed and shouted, and measured the length of the welcome stranger, calculating how much he weighed, and how many he would feed.

"He weighs just forty pounds, over or under," said Boreas. "I have been in the trade, and can judge within a few ounces."

"There's another at the hook, Captain," said Flora, who was holding the line. "Pull it in—I am not able."

"By Jove! so there is. And hullo! the shoemakers will beat us, if we don't take care—see, they are getting one in bigger than ours—a perfect buster! If it is sinful to take these creature comforts, we are very thankful to God for his mercy in sending them," glancing with his one eye hard at the preacher.

"It is sin, great and heinous sin," said that individual, in his sepulchral voice; "and I think it my duty to denounce such iniquity."

"You are welcome to do so, if it affords you any amusement," returned Boreas, hauling up another great fish upon the deck, and coolly re-baiting his hook; "but I would thank you to stand back and mind your own business."

"It's my duty, man of sin, to warn you of your danger, and tell these ill-advised people not to follow your evil example."

"Tol-de-rol!" said Boreas, snapping his fingers, and casting his line overboard. "Our blessed Lord, when He was hungry, gathered ears of corn and ate them, on the Sabbath-day. I and my people are starving, and we fish to obtain food to preserve us and these little ones"—pointing to the children—"alive. And now, Sir, you have had your answer."

The preacher regarded him with a sullen scowl, and turned away—but not without sundry threatenings of Divine vengeance, "which he was certain," he affirmed, "would follow his wicked proceedings. And you, Madam," he continued, addressing himself to Flora, "I am surprised to see you, who ought to know better, not only abetting this man in his iniquitous proceedings by your presence, but actually participating in his guilt!"

"If I thought he was acting wrong, Mr. S——," said Flora, "I should not be here. But I consider that he is engaged in a good work, which God has sanctioned, by giving us the food we sought."

"A false and worldly conclusion, which will be followed by the same punishment that befel the rebellious Israelites in the wilderness, when they lusted for strange food."

"The case is somewhat different. Their daily food, though distasteful to them, was constantly supplied; but some of these people have no food at all."

"They deserve to starve, for their disobedience and want of faith!"

"When our stores are exhausted," said Boreas, "those who are *well* supplied must contribute their stock for the general benefit. We shall not starve alone."

"How, Sir!—Do you expect the prudent to give up their substance to the idle and the improvident?"

This was said with much asperity of look and tone.

"Hunger knows no law—respects no property. In cases of general distress, men claim all things in common, and become Communists in downright earnest. While your locker contains a single biscuit, you will be called upon to share it with the rest."

Mr. S—— made no answer to this speech, and walked sullenly away.

Before noon, the Captain and the Muckleroys had forty noble fish lying upon the deck. Thirty of these, the Captain had caught with his own hand.

"This is a fine sight," he said. "We have reason to thank God for this great mercy, in spite of all yon sour-faced sulky fellow may say to the contrary. He may satisfy his stomach with beef and biscuit—not a morsel of this fresh fish shall rejoice the cockles of his heart."

"Not so, Captain," said Flora. "Let us test the sincerity of his profession by sending him one of these fish as his share of the spoil, and see whether his practice is equal to his professions of superior sanctity."

"Faith, you are right! But he will never be such a d——d hypocrite as to accept it!"

"Try him."

"What shall I bet that he will send it back, with a long sermon tacked to its tail?"

"Don't bet; you would be sure to lose; that is, if I judge that man's physiognomy rightly. There is nothing good or benevolent in his face; and the face, after all, is the map of the mind."

"Well, I'll send it, just to please you. Here, Sam Fraser, take this fish to Mr. S——, with my compliments."

Sam went, and returned with a comic smile on his face.

"Well, Sam, did he condescend to take the wages of our iniquity?"

"Ay, Sir, and returns you his *best* thanks. He has given Geordie Muckleroy a shilling to clean the fish for him, though it is Sunday. I think if you watch the stove, he will be cooking it himself before long."

"The devil he will! Mrs. Lyndsay, you are a witch. I could have taken my oath that he would not have touched it with a pair of tongs."

"Captain, you know little of human nature."

"But the fellow is so religious."

"So fanatical, you should say. That man never felt the sweet influences of Christianity. He deals in words—not deeds. See, here he comes! with a piece of the fresh fish to broil for his dinner. Let us go down into the cabin; the sight of us might chance to spoil his appetite."[C]

[C] A fact.

CHAPTER XXV
THE STORM

For several days after the fishing adventure, Flora was confined to her berth with severe indisposition, and was, indeed, so alarmingly ill, that at one time she thought that she would be consigned to the deep, as food for the fishes, on the great banks of Newfoundland. She loathed the bad water and food, and became so much reduced by sickness, that poor little Josey had to be weaned.

It was a great blessing that the young, tender creature, suffered little from the privation. She ate her meals of biscuit softened in the putrid water, with an appetite that health and hunger alone can give, and looked as rosy and as happy upon the coarse diet prepared by the kind and attentive Sam Fraser, as if it had been compounded of the finest white bread and new milk.

"Oh, what a blessing it is, my darling, that you continue so well!" said Flora, on the fourth morning after her baby's natural sustenance had been withdrawn. "I thought this illness would have been the death of you."

"Dinna distress yersel about the wean," said Mrs. Muckleroy; "the gude God takes care o' His ain. The wee cherub is as blithe as a lark. The pure, fresh air, is baith meat an' drink to her."

Fortunately for Flora, the Captain had a consignment of old port on board, a couple of tablespoonfuls of which, mixed with a little oatmeal, twice a day, was all the nourishment she was able to take; but, in all probability, it was the means of saving her life, and preventing her from sinking from utter exhaustion.

When once more able to leave her bed and crawl upon deck, she looked the mere shadow of her former self. The women, with whom she was a great favourite, crowded round her to shake her by the hand, and offer their congratulations on her recovery. Their simple and affectionate expressions of regard and sympathy moved her very much.

"What depths of kindness there is in the human heart!" she thought. "How little do we understand and appreciate the minds of uneducated people, whom we are too apt to look down upon as inferiors. How far they surpass the hackneyed children of the world in their generous devotion to those they love. Unfettered by conventional selfishness, they dare to obey the natural instincts of their humanity—to act and think with simplicity and truth. We mistrust them, because we are unacquainted with their mode of life, and the motives which influence their general conduct. They look up to us, and have boundless faith in the superiority of our position and intelligence. When will a higher Christianity than that which at present rules the world break down the wall which pride and bigotry have raised between children descended from one parent stock, and bridge the gulf of poverty and ignorance that now separates them from each other?"

"The time is coming," cries the philanthropic speculator; but adds, with a sigh, "it will not be in our day. Yet it will surely come."

Three weeks the ship had been becalmed upon the banks, the dull monotony of the dreary fog only relieved by the ringing of a large bell and the blowing of horns, which were kept up at regular intervals during the day and night, in order to prevent the ship being run down by some larger vessel.

At length the morning came which brought a fair wind to fill the sails of the *Anne*; and her passengers looked up to the blue heavens, and blessed the light of the sun. Joy and hope again beamed from every face. The little brown man's morose aspect alone remained unchanged.

The tall, lithe figure of Mr. Collins seemed to have grown two inches higher, as he paced the deck with elastic steps and head erect. The little tailor was at his post among the clouds at the mast-head, seeing visions of green fields, and singing like a lark; Stephen Corrie was in an ecstasy of mirth; and Tam Grant could not cross the deck without cutting sundry mad capers which set all the rest laughing.

The women crept from their hiding-place in the dark depths of the steerage, and sat smoking their black short pipes, and chatting in lively tones to each other. Even Granny Williamson forgot to quarrel with her daughter, and mounted a clean mutch on the occasion; the soldier Mackenzie, to scold his diminutive wife; or Mistress Macdonald, to annoy the Captain with threats of maternity, and bully her husband. The Sultan of the deck—the dour Boreas himself—resigned for once his dignity, and condescended to laugh and chat, and draw agreeable presages of the future, from the fair wind and the smiling day.

Flora felt tranquilly happy, as she sat on a camp stool upon the deck, with Josey nestled in her arms, and old Oscar basking in the warm sun at her feet, rejoicing in the change which a few hours had made in their prospects. The very waves that followed in their wake, and curled around their prow, flashing and leaping in the sunlight, seemed to lift up their voices and utter a strain of joyful merriment, in having escaped the thrall of the dull, lethargic mist, which had so long held them in silence and inactivity. Yesterday, and not a breath of air stirred the leaden surface of the sea. No glance from the sun's bright eye looked down upon them through the blinding, wildering white veil, suspended between them and heaven. The mist penetrated every where—it hid the sails, floated above the cold, damp, slippery deck, and entered the very cabin, chilling their hearts with apathy and gloom.

Nature had suddenly started from her mesmeric trance, and was wide awake once more; and all the human hearts imprisoned in the *Anne* responded to her electric touch. The very ship seemed endowed with living power, and bounded over the long rolling surges as if she felt the impetus of the fresh wind which filled her canvas in all her creaking timbers.

"This is glorious, Captain: shall we soon clear the banks?"

"We left them behind two hours ago."

"Shall we see land before night?"

He shook his head. "It's not in the breeks of the *Anne*. She is old, and slow in her paces. With the same wind, we shall be fortunate if we do so to-morrow."

Flora went to bed, hoping and praying for the fair wind to continue, and fill their sails on the morrow.

The morrow came, and filled its appointed place in the long annals of time; and still the ship held on her course, with the same blue skies above, and the same blue desert of ocean, limitless and vast, around.

The nearer they approached the desired haven, the more contradictory and morose Mr. Lootie became. The hope which inspired all with a flutter of joyful anticipation, seemed to awaken no feelings of gratitude and thankfulness in him. He grumbled and snarled at every one and every thing.

At noon, a vessel hove in sight. It was the first that had crossed their long and lonely path; and as she drew near, every one rushed to the deck to look at the stranger. She passed so near, that there was but a narrow path of waves between them; and her crew, in red flannel shirts and worsted caps, seemed as much swayed by the excitement of the moment, as the half-starved passengers on board the *Anne*.

The Captain bellowed through his trumpet to enquire her name, port, and destination, as she glided by, and was answered, in the same trumpet tones—

"The barque *Mary* of London, Captain Jones; freight, timber; ten days from Quebec—all well!"

In a few minutes she was gone, soon to become a mere speck on the horizon.

Flora turned with a sigh, from following her track along the deep. She was going home, and the very thought of that distant, never-to-be-forgotten home, flooded her heart with sad memories.

"Don't look so grave, Mrs. Lyndsay," said old Boreas. "In ten days we may reach Quebec. I hear Sam ringing the bell for dinner. I thought I would give you a little treat, and have ordered the cook to prepare for us a dog's body."

"A dog's body!—Captain, you could not be so cruel!" She glanced round the deck. Oscar was lying near her, his red eyes gleaming affectionately upon her through his tangled locks. "You have not, surely, ordered the poor Northumbrian's brindled slut to be killed, to give a taste of fresh meat?"

"Why not?" said Boreas, with a grin. "To be sure, she is not in prime condition. But those three fine pups of hers are as fat as butter. The Chinese eat dog, and why should not we?"

"You are not in earnest!"

"Ask Sam."

Flora was perplexed. She saw a smile on Lyndsay's face, and went to Oscar's kennel to ascertain the fact.

Now Oscar, who had three times saved the Captain's life, rejoiced in a fine greenhouse, which stood near the companion-ladder, and was taken as much care of as any of the crew. The brindled slut had thought fit to appropriate this handsome berth to herself, in which she had a fortnight before brought forth three fine bull-dog pups, which Flora had christened Triton, Boatswain, and Neptune.

Oscar had manifested the utmost indignation at this appropriation of his property. He had tried to expel the female invader of his rights with the most awful threats of vengeance, in the shape of snarls, barks, and ferocious growls. But Madame Brindle had claimed the law of the strongest, and, without having consulted Blackstone on the subject, had found out that possession is nine parts of the law.

For a whole day Oscar had endeavoured to effect an ejectment; but the brindled slut had very calmly looked out at the door and laughed at his impotent rage, to the no small amusement of Flora. Oscar at length abandoned the contest in disgust, and not only left Madame Brindle in possession, but disdained to go near his old domicile, in which his foe made herself quite at home, with her bottle-nosed family.

Flora peeped into the kennel, but Brindle had curled herself up for a comfortable nap, and did not choose to be disturbed.

"I am glad he has not killed you, poor beast," said Flora; "but I don't see the pups," and, full of anxiety, she followed the Captain down to dinner.

The laugh was now against her; for the dog's body turned out to be a pease pudding, of which she ate very heartily, while Boreas rubbed his hands, and chuckled at the joke.

To while away the tedium of the voyage, she and Lyndsay would take it by turns to play draughts with the Captain. They always were the victors. He did not mind being beat by Lyndsay, but his pride was deeply mortified, whenever Flora won the game.

"A man may beat a man," he would grumble out, "but, d—— it, I don't like being thrashed by a woman. Mrs. Lyndsay, you have no right to beat a sailor on his own deck, at checkers."

The Captain was by no means a bad-hearted man; but he had many odd peculiarities. One of these was his insisting on keeping his pipe in the large, flat-bottomed, greasy candlestick. This afternoon he missed it from its usual place.

"Sam!" he thundered, in his stentorian voice—"Sam Fraser!—What the devil have you done with my pipe?"

"It's in the cupboard, Sir," said Sam, obsequiously.

"How dared you put it in the cupboard, when I had found out such a *clean* place for it?"

"Why, Sir,—I thought, Sir, the cupboard was the best place for it."

"You thought! Sir, you have no business to think, without I give you leave. If I had put it in the pitch-pot, you had no right to take it out, unordered by me!"

Sam bowed with the gravity of a judge, handing him the black, greasy pipe, with the deference due from a subject to his sovereign prince.

The Captain had lost his eye in a storm, in which his ship (not the *Anne*) had suffered wreck. He had effected his escape through the cabin-window, and a splinter of the glass had pierced his eye and destroyed his sight. This was one of the occasions in which he had been saved by the faithful Oscar, who kept him above water until a boat picked him up. The splinter of glass was afterwards extracted by the surgeon of a man-of-war; and Boreas kept it in a snuff-box, which he always carried about his person, and looked upon it in the light of a charm.

"While I can keep this and Oscar," he said, "I shall never suffer from shipwreck again."

It would have been a difficult matter for any one to persuade him to part with the one or the other of these precious relics.

A great many private letters had been entrusted to his care. This was against the law. Boreas was aware of the fact, and took advantage of it. Every dull day, Sundays especially, he brought these letters from the depths of his huge sea-chest, and amused himself by spelling them over, until he must have learned their contents by heart.

Lyndsay remonstrated with him on this dishonourable conduct.

"Hout! man," he said, "the writers of these letters cheated the Government in sending them by me. It just serves them right. I shall read them as often as I please."

This fact should be a useful hint to persons who, for the sake of saving a trifling amount of postage, entrust letters of consequence to private hands. These letters never reached their destination. After having afforded entertainment to this rough seaman during the voyage, they were thrown overboard before the vessel arrived at Quebec.

The next day the wind still continued fair, but the weather was hazy, and sultry hot. The Captain promised the first man who should descry land a dollar, and a double allowance of grog.

"I'll bet upon the little tailor," he cried, as he saw Sandy mounting with alacrity to his lofty perch. "That fellow has a great soul, though he wears a small pair of breeks. There's luck in his sharp face and keen eye."

James Hawke determined not to be outdone by the tailor, and took up an exalted position on the mast, while the rest of the passengers walked to and fro the deck, straining their eyes, and looking in all directions for the promised land. A bank of dull grey clouds obscured the distant horizon, and for some time they looked in vain.

A warm resinous smell came at times upon the wind, and large masses of sea-weed floated continually past. Flora was watching these with great interest, when the little brown man, who had kept quiet for some days, sauntered to her side.

He was in a more contradictory mood than ever.

"A fine day, Mrs. Lyndsay."

"Rather hazy.—It looks like rain."

"*Quite* the reverse. The sky is *quite* clear."

"Independent of that fog-bank."

"*Fog!* I see no *fog*. You are blind, my dear Madam. The atmosphere is *unusually* clear."

Flora stared at him. "Could the man be in his senses?" Presently she remarked, "that they must be near land, from the quantity of sea-weed floating upon the water."

"*That's* not sea-weed!"

"Mr. Lootie, I was born and brought up on the sea-coast: don't you think I know sea-weed?"

"Not if you call pieces of reed and grass *sea-weed*. And as to being *near* land, that's all fudge. The Captain only says so to please you."

Lyndsay, who was standing near, now took Flora's arm, and walked to the other side of the deck. "What a little contradictory, snarling creature it is!" he said. "Why do you bandy words with him? Look, here is a piece of twisted paper. I will go forward, and throw it overboard. It looks like nothing but what it is. You return to Lootie, and when it passes, say, 'There's a piece of white paper,' and just hear how he will contradict the fact."

Flora did as she was told.

Presently the paper floated just beneath the spot where they were standing.

"Ah!" cries Flora, with feigned surprise, "we must be near land. See—there is a piece of white paper."

"Pshaw! *Paper indeed!* where are your eyes? It is a *feather*—a white *feather*, belonging to some sea-fowl or other."

"A *goosle*, perhaps, Mr. Lootie. But no, it is what I say, a piece of paper."

"A *feather*, Madam, a *feather*!"

"Why, there's writing upon it; I see the letters."

"Nonsense, it is a *feather*, speckled with black and grey. I'll swear it's a feather !" and his shrill voice rose almost to a scream.

Lyndsay joined the disputants, hardly able to keep from laughing in the face of the angry little elf. "Flora, did you see the piece of paper I flung overboard just now? I thought it would set you wondering?"

"Now, Mr. Lootie, what do you say to your *feather*?"

"That I hate senseless jokes, and the fools who make them," snarled the ex-distiller, as he retired with a face as black as a thunder-cloud.

About four in the afternoon, the clouds cleared away, the sun came out brilliantly, and the cry of "Land! land, to the left!" was sung out lustily from the mast-head.

The little tailor had won the promised reward, and it was not many minutes before he reached the deck to claim it.

Land was indeed in sight, not exactly that which they looked for. The ship was considerably out of the usual track, and was rather too near for safety, to the stern mountain peak of Cape Breton. The Captain calculated it to be about fourteen miles distant before sunset, and the dark outline of rock and forest was visible to the naked eye.

It was a warm, delicious summer evening, and the smell of the pine forests was as rich as gales of Araby to the poor emigrants. The Captain had treated all hands to a stiff glass of grog; and the Duncans had tuned their fiddles, and young and old were assembled upon the deck for a dance.

Flora was too much entranced with the sight of land, to heed the dancers as they bounded past; shouting and laughing in their mad revel of mirth.

The moon had risen above the frowning Cape, and flooded the land and sea with light. The jollity of the passengers and crew profaned the calm grandeur of the night—the august and profound solitude of sea and sky. Gladly would she have shut out all such sights and sounds, to commune with her own heart, with nature, and with nature's God, while gazing upon such a scene, at such an hour. "But fast and furious grew the fun," and a cry from her babe, whom she had left sleeping in her little cabin, faint as it was, reached her maternal ear; and she left the revellers, to attend to the wants of her child.

Josey was fretful and restless, and more than an hour elapsed before she could hush her again to sleep. She was still lying beside her on her berth, with the little creature's arms clasped tightly about her neck, when the ship seemed to reel and lurch, as if suddenly struck by a tremendous blow. Then came shouts and cries—the trampling of feet, the creaking of ropes and chains; and still the ship plunged and tossed, with such a violent motion, that she had to hold to the berth to keep her feet. What could all this mean?—was she in a dream? Everything was bright and beautiful above, when she quitted the deck. Whence then came the confusion of sounds—the hoarse roaring of winds—the dashing of waves—the fearful tossing to and fro of her ocean home? Flora gently unclasped the clinging arms of her sleeping babe, and groping her way through the dark cabin, with great difficulty succeeded in climbing the companion-ladder, and bringing her head on a level with the deck.

She did not venture higher. She saw enough to convince her that women had no place amid the horrors of such an awful scene. A sudden squall from the mountains had struck the ship. The moon had withdrawn her light; and vast masses of clouds covered the sky, which was before so clear and brilliant. Vast sheets of foam enveloped the vessel, and huge billows thundered upon her deck. Not a stitch of canvas was to be seen; some of the sails had been rent from the mast by the gale; the rest were close furled. Lyndsay and four other men were at the rudder, to keep the ship in her course. The roaring of the winds and waves was deafening. Flora's heart beat violently for a moment, then grew calm before the grandeur of the scene.

"We are in the hands of God!" she thought; "in life and death we are His. Submission to His will is the sublimity of faith!"

In the cabin everything was loose. Trunks rolled from side to side. The mate had removed the light, and utter darkness prevailed. It was a long time before she could regain her little domicile—the ship pitched with such violence, that every step brought her to her knees; at length she found the door, and lifting the mattress from her berth, into which she found it impossible to climb, she took her baby in her arms, and lay down upon the heaving floor, commending herself and her fellow-passengers to the care of God.

To sleep was impossible; but her mind seemed sustained by a lofty courage which made her feel calm in the midst of danger. This strength was not her own; it was derived from a higher source—a firm reliance on the unerring wisdom and providence of God. If death was His decree, she would try to meet it with becoming fortitude. Resistance and lamentations were alike useless; even prayers for self-preservation appeared impious. She was in His keeping, and she felt confident that whatever might befal her and those so dear to her was for the best.

The hurricane roared through the long starless night. Floods of rain forced their way through the skylight, and drenched her bed. She buried her head in the wet blankets, and shivered with cold. Yet Josey slept as peacefully as ever on her mother's breast, happily unconscious of the terrors of the hour.

About four o'clock in the morning, Lyndsay opened the door of her little cabin. The water was streaming from his garments.

"Flora, are you awake?"

"Yes, darling," she cried, starting to a sitting posture; "who could sleep in such a storm?"

"It has been a dreadful night. The danger is over. The ship is no longer on the lee shore, but standing out to sea. At one time, we expected that she would run upon the rocks and go down. The gale still continues, but we have plenty of sea-room. I have been hard at work all night. The men behaved like trumps—especially old Macdonald and the Dragoon. I am going to change these wet clothes, and lie down for an hour. So content yourself, my Flora. Thank God for our deliverance, and go to sleep."

Flora had silently done that already. In a few minutes she was slumbering as peacefully as Josey—dreaming of green fields, and running brooks, and wandering with dear familiar faces, among nature's quiet haunts, in the memory-haunting eternity of the past.

CHAPTER XXVI
THE SHIP COMES TO AN ANCHOR, AND THE BOOK TO A CLOSE

The next morning, Flora hastened upon deck; but while there, the wind was still so high, and the waves so rough, that she could not stand without holding to the ropes. The sea was covered with foam, the heavens with flying rack, which rolled in huge broken masses round and round the horizon. The land was no longer in sight, and old ocean roared and tossed in his unrest, as a strong man raves and tosses in the delirium of fever.

"The white mice are out this morning, Mrs. Lyndsay," said Bob Motion, who was at his old post at the helm. "Miss Josey's cradle, I'm thinking, was well rocked last night. We are now running right afore the gale. The skipper was out of his reckoning altogether. It's a mercy the ship did not founder on that cursed shore."

At noon the storm abated, with a fair wind.

"If this lasts, we shall have a glorious run," said Mr. Collins, laying down his knife and fork at dinner, "and shall most likely get clear of Anticosti before morning."

They passed this dangerous island during the night.

"I am sorry," said Flora, "that we did not see it."

"You should rather thank God, Mrs. Lyndsay; but don't be too sure—we may see too much of it yet."

The Captain's words were prophetic. Three days of stormy weather and contrary winds found the vessel tossing between Charleroi Bay and the dismal coast, whose dreary aspect sailors view with such fear. The setting sun shone upon the white rocky cliffs of Cape Gaspé, and the fantastic rocks which surround that romantic bay; and his rising beams gleamed upon the sandy beach and desolate shores of Anticosti, with its grey forests of storm-stunted trees of horrid growth, that looked the fitting abode of the savage bear and wolf.

In Chaleur Bay they caught some fresh fish, which was indeed a seasonable mercy, as it had become painfully evident that their stock of provisions could not hold out many days longer.

On the 25th of August they took in a pilot off Cape Rosier, who brought some fresh provisions in his boat, and the fearful intelligence, that the cholera was raging at Quebec, and spreading into the Upper Province.

This piece of information threw a damp upon the spirits of all. They had escaped the dangers of the sea, only to encounter the more terrible peril of the pestilence. "What must be, must—we all know that," said Boreas. "No man that knows me would call me a coward; but I'll confess the truth—I'm afraid of this infernal cholera; I'll be d—— if I aren't."

Every one had some prophetic fear or foreboding on the subject. Persons who had not trembled during the storm, turned pale and shuddered when the pestilence was named.

Geordie Muckleroy alone seemed perfectly indifferent about it. "That man's sic a muckle sumph, he's no afeard o' onything," said Mrs. Mackenzie, the dragoon's little drunken wife. "The night o' the storm he must put his heid above the gangway to spier about it; and sic a glour as he gied at the sea, I'se never forget to my deein day. 'What's a' this muckle din?' quo' he. 'Why, man, we are a' like to be drown'd in the salt brine. It's an awfu' storm,' said my husband—'Come up, an' lend a han' wi' the ropes.'"

"'The deil may tak' the ropes for what I care,' quo' he; 'I'll no fash mysel' about ropes, or ony thin' else, the night. I'll jest gang awa' comfortably to my ain bed, an' tak' it easy.' An' to bed he went, sure eneugh, though his puir wife was tearing her hair, an' skirlin' for fear, the hale night."

The pilot, among the stores he brought on board, had nothing so tempting to Flora as a box of raisins, which Lyndsay purchased for her, and which were opened for the benefit of all in the cabin.

"You had better put those things out of sight, they'll give you the cholera," said Boreas. "They wouldn't be so bad in a pudding," he continued musingly—"Suppose you give some of them to Hanibal, to make into a plum-pudding. There is some flour left; it's a little musty, to be sure, but hungry dogs—you know the rest."

Flora piqued herself on making a good plum-pudding; she volunteered to prepare it for the cook, and Sam Fraser provided her with flour, water, and a board and pudding bag.

"I want eggs, Sam."

"Eggs, Ma'am?—no eggs to be had."

"Milk."

"The cow arn't calved that' to pervide that."

"Well, get me some suet."

"None in the ship. Only a little rancid butter."

"Take away the flour and the board. The idea of making a plum-pudding out of putrid water, musty flour, and raisins, is too ridiculous."

."Give me some of the raisins," said Sam, "and Hanibal will make a sea plum-pudding."

"I wonder what it will be like!" And Flora laughed, as she gave him as many raisins as he required.

It was amusing to watch the Captain at dinner, playing the petty tyrant over the poor French pilot, on to whose plate he chucked the outside slice of the hard, tough beef, as if he had been throwing a bone to a dog.

The pilot showed his white teeth, and his dark eyes blazed as he flashed them full in the Captain's face, and, throwing the meat back into the dish, he strode from the table.

"Brother," said Collins, a name he seldom applied to the Captain, and only when he wished to impress him particularly on any important subject, "you had better try anither tack wi' the pilot. That won't do. He's a proud, high-spirited fellow; he'll no stand ony nonsense."

"He may sit it, then. I'll treat him as I please."

"Then he'll leave you to navigate the St. Lawrence alone."

The Captain shrugged his shoulders, and said nothing.

"Let me ca' him back to the table, and apologise."

"Call him back if you like; but, d—— the apology!"

"I'll mak' it straight," cried Collins; and, leaving the cabin, he soon returned with the Frenchman, followed by Sam and the sea-pudding, who, placing it before the Captain with a most impressive air, looked triumphantly across the table at Mrs. Lyndsay.

"A nice piece of duff that, Sam," said Boreas, striking his knife and fork into the fair sides of the jolly white pudding.

"Wery nice, Sir," responded Sam.

"This your manufacturing, Mrs. L.?"

Flora shook her head.—"I was not going to disgrace the national dish by compounding it of such materials."

"You have been stingy of the plums, Sam. They are scarcely within hail of each other."

"He should have told the cook to whistle while he was picking them," said Flora, laughing. "I gave out plenty for a large, rich pudding."

"I'll help the youngsters first," said Boreas, handing a large slice to James Hawke; "boys love duff."

The first mouthful was enough for poor Jim. He made a horrid face, and pushed back his plate.

"Hey! what's the matter with the lad?"

"Oh!" said Jim, hurrying from the table. "I shall never be able to eat plum-pudding again."

The pudding looked so clean and nice, that Flora was tempted to taste it. She no longer wondered at the boy's disgust. It was made with rancid fat, bad water, and boiled in the sea-brine. To a stomach unaccustomed to such dainties, it was unpalatable in the highest degree. Yet the Captain, Mate, and Pilot ate of it, and pronounced it excellent.

"I knew how it would be," said Flora; "and yet I am baby enough to be disappointed at the result."

"The child has quarrelled with its pudding," said Boreas, "and left more for us. It's an ill wind that blows no one any good."

"Pray don't call it my pudding, Captain. I disown it altogether. There is nothing English about it."

Hannah, who had recovered her health and usefulness in a miraculous manner, since her master's quarrel with the Captain, at any rate showed an English appetite while discussing the execrable mess. Flora, who was really hungry, and longing for wholesome food, envied her the zest with which she demolished slice after slice, and still kept sending up her plate for more.

That night they were given an awful specimen of a Canadian thunder-storm. The atmosphere was literally a-blaze with the lightning, while heaven's dread artillery burst continuously overhead, the long mountain-chain, on the north side of the river, hurling it back from all its rocky caverns in one deep unbroken round.

It was a night of awful and terrific beauty. Flora had never beheld its parallel in the old country—had never seen such electric flashes of blinding light, nor heard such ear-splitting peals of thunder. For the first time their dangerous freight flashed upon her mind; she remembered the gunpowder, and clung closer to the arm of her husband.

"See how the lightning plays upon the iron rings and bolts which fasten the sails to the mast—what if it should strike the ship, dear John?"

"Don't anticipate evil, Flora. There may be danger, but as we can neither escape from it, nor avert it, if it comes, it is better not to dwell upon it."

"It would be a bad job for us a'," said Mr. Collins. "But if it sud happen, we should be blown to pieces with the ship, an' ken nothing about it. I canna imagine an easier death."

"The very suddenness of it makes it appear to me so dreadful," said Flora. "It is not pleasant to know that you are standing over a volcano, which one spark might ignite, and scatter you in fragments into the air and waters. Are these storms common in Canada?"

"I dinna ken," returned Collins; "this is my first voyage."

"They are of frequent occurrence, Mrs. Lyndsay," said Mr. Wright, who happened to be passing, "and are often accompanied with dreadful hurricanes, that sweep down every thing which obstructs their course. The awful fire at Miramichi, which took place a few years ago, and which burnt up half the forests in the country, was supposed to have been kindled by lightning. I happened to be there at the time; and though staying in a cleared part of the country, with a relation of my wife, the appearance that the fire made was so terrible that it often haunts me in dreams."

The cabin was so close, and the lightning so vivid, that Flora, in spite of the rain, preferred walking the deck until the storm subsided, which it did before day-break, when she retired to bed,

"And sleep protracted came with double power."

The next day brought both the beautiful shores of the St. Lawrence in sight, and Flora remained chained to her post on the deck from morning until night; her eyes never weary of dwelling upon the glorious river, its romantic islands, and magnificent banks.

What a noble panorama the St. Lawrence would make—to follow all the windings of this matchless stream, from Grosse Ile, through its chain of inland seas! Perhaps no country in the world could present finer subjects for such a work; with water so pure—skies so blue—rock, mountain and forest so vast—and cities, towns and villages along its shores placed in such picturesque and imposing situations. A pictorial map of Canada could alone give a just idea of the beauty and importance of this great country to the good folks at home. Then consider the adjuncts of such a landscape—the falls of Montmorency, and God's masterpiece, Niagara. The panorama of its Upper and Lower Mississippi would lose half their beauty, when contrasted with the panorama of the St. Lawrence, with its tumultuous rapids and thousand isles.

An old friend of Mrs. Lyndsay, who had visited almost every country, had assured her that nothing he had ever seen during his travels through the world surpassed in grandeur and beauty the shores of the St. Lawrence, Rio Janeiro alone excepted; and so well had he described every remarkable scene on their passage up the river, that Flora instantly recognised the spot from the vivid pictures he had given her of them from memory.

How she longed to land upon the lovely islands which continually glided past them! Some of these were partly cultivated, and neat white farm-houses peeped out from the midst of orchards glowing with ripe fruits, and the first gorgeous tints of the Canadian fall. On the south shores of the river, the wheat was still standing in the sheaf upon the yellow uplands, and the forest and the harvest changing colour, and blending their rich hues into a splendid harmony of the bright and beautiful. As if to atone for the long, cold winter (and yet how charming that winter is!) Nature puts on royal robes to cover her decay; and autumn, which in other countries is so melancholy and sober in her russet dress, is, in Canada, the most attractive and delightful season of the four. Who does not prefer it to the warm, humid, leafless spring?—to the blazing sun, cloudless skies, and enervating heat of summer?—or to the cold, bright blue and silver sheen of the spotless winter?

On the 29th of August they passed Crane Island, the beautiful domain of Mr. Macpherson, on the north side of the river; and early on the morning of the 30th, the *Anne* cast her anchor opposite Grosse Ile.

And here we shall leave our emigrants, in the bustle, confusion, and excitement of preparing to go on shore, having described the voyage from thence to Quebec and up the St. Lawrence elsewhere.

If any of my readers should feel interested in the fate of the Lyndsays, we will briefly add, by way of postscript, all we know concerning them.

The Lyndsays settled upon wild land, and suffered, for some years, great hardships in the Backwoods. Ultimately Mr. Lyndsay obtained an official appointment, which enabled him to remove his wife and family to one of the fast-rising and flourishing towns of the Upper Province, where they have since resided in great happiness and comfort, and no longer regret their voyage to Canada, but bless the kind Providence which led them hither.

As an illustration of that protecting and merciful interposition, so often manifested by the Great Father to his dependent children, we must here add, that the two disastrous trips to sea related in the former part of these volumes, by preventing the Lyndsays from taking passage to Canada in the *Chieftain*, in all probability were the means of preserving them from falling victims to the cholera, as all the passengers in that unfortunate vessel perished with the fatal epidemic.

The *Rachel*, the ship to which Flora felt such an unconquerable objection, was wrecked upon the banks of Newfoundland, after having been twelve weeks at sea. The Captain was made a prisoner, and confined during the greater part of the voyage to his cabin by his brutal sons, while many of her passengers died of small-pox and want of food.

How kind, then, was the Providence that watched over our poor emigrants; although, like the rest of the world, they were tempted to murmur at the provoking delay, nor could discover the beam in the dark cloud, until the danger was past, and they had leisure to reflect upon the great perils they had escaped, and the mercies they had received from the Almighty Disposer of all human destinies.

Musa, King of Grenada, owed his elevation to the throne to a delay of five minutes: when he requested the executioner, whom his jealous brother had sent to the prison to take his head, to allow him that brief space until he had checkmated the gaoler, with whom he was playing a game at chess, the grim official reluctantly consented. Before the time expired, a tumult in the city dethroned his brother, and gave Musa his crown. How much he owed to that one move at chess! Could that be merely accidental, on which the fate of a nation and the lives of thousands were staked?

So with the Lyndsays. The storm—the fog—the lost passage in the *Chieftain*—the presentiment against sailing in the *Rachel*—though apparently *very trifling* circumstances, formed most important links in their destiny. Reader, have faith in Providence. A good father is never indifferent to the welfare of his child—still less a merciful God!